INDIAN NO MORE

INDIAN NO MORE

By Charlene Willing McManis
with Traci Sorell

TU BOOKS

An Imprint of Lee & Low Books Inc.
New York

Text and photographs copyright © 2019 by Charlene Willing McManis and
Traci Sorell

TU BOOKS, an imprint of LEE & LOW BOOKS Inc.,
95 Madison Avenue, New York, NY 10016
leeandlow.com

Manufactured in the United States of America

MIX
Paper from
responsible sources
FSC® C002589

Cover art by Marlena Myles
Title hand lettering by Michelle Cunningham
Map illustration © 2019 by Tim Paul Piotrowski
Edited by Elise McMullen-Ciotti and Stacy Whitman
Typesetting by ElfElm Publishing
Book production by The Kids at Our House
The text is set in Garamond No. 3

10 9 8 7 6 5 4 3 2
First Edition

Cataloging-in-Publication Data is on file with the Library of Congress

For all the Native Nations and their citizens
who suffered the terrible impact of termination
and relocation.

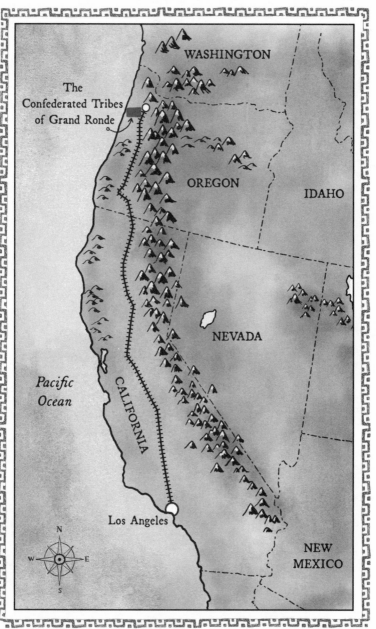

A NOTE FOR READERS

Indian No More focuses on an Umpqua family in the 1950s and includes both words and sayings in Chinuk Wawa—the language of The Confederated Tribes of Grand Ronde—and a number of historical references. If you would like help with or want to know more about anything you encounter in the text, please check the list of Chinuk Wawa words below or the glossary and pronunciation guide on page 171. Thank you for reading.

GLOSSARY

Chich (chitch): grandmother

Chinuk Wawa (chah-nook wah-wah): a jargon used by tribes in the Pacific Northwest to communicate and trade with one another. The nearly thirty tribes that form The Confederated Tribes of the Grand Ronde Community spoke various languages, so the use of Chinuk Wawa helped everyone be able to speak and interact with one another after their forced removals by the federal government to the reservation.

Chup (choop): grandfather

kʰwiʔim (kwa-eem): grandchild

kʰəpít (kah-bit): Stop!

miməlust·ʳ (mee-maah-loos): to die

saχali-tayi (sah-HAH-lee tah-ee): Grandfather or High-up Chief, similar to God

tənəs-man (tuh-nas-mon): son

t'siyatkʰu·ʳ (tsee-yat-koo): a tall, hairy creature that lives in the coastal woods, often referred to as Sasquatch or Bigfoot in English

wawa-laχayam·ʳ kitəp-san·ʳ (wah-wah thlah-hyam kah-bit-saan): to greet the sunrise

TABLE OF CONTENTS

1

THE WALKING DEAD

Before being terminated, I was Indian.

Now I certainly don't mean I was killed off or anything. It was 1954. The United States government didn't do that anymore. They just filed away our tribal roll numbers. Erased our reservation from the map.

What were our tribal roll numbers? They were the numbers the tribe assigned to its citizens and used by the federal government to see who belonged to the tribe. So my number verified that I was Regina Petit (roll number 3669), daughter of John Petit (roll number 858), granddaughter of Maude Petit (roll number 25) and Sid Petit (roll number 18).

And that was what made you Indian to the US government—numbers.

Even after all that counting, the government chose to terminate us. I really don't know all the reasons why, but my chich, my grandmother, said this much: "Termination means we're the walking dead."

Now I ask you, how can we be dead if we're still walking?

2
REZ LIFE

But I'm getting ahead of myself. Let me start at the beginning. I was born on the Grand Ronde Indian Reservation, just over thirty miles west from the state capital in Salem, Oregon. I had lived there all my life. I didn't know any way to live other than as an Umpqua Indian. My family was Umpqua. I was Umpqua. That was just how it was.

Living on the rez, I played outside with my younger sister Peewee. (Her given name was Theresa, but nobody except our school teacher ever called her that.) We ate wild blackberries and plucked blue larkspurs without any adults watching. Ours was a small reservation compared to others in Oregon. My people didn't bother the whites that lived around us. Our rez owned a cramped trailer that housed our health and dental clinic, a post office that used to be someone's house, and an "everything you need from canned beans to carpenter nails" store on the corner of Highway 22 and Grand Ronde Road.

My elementary school was painted yellow, and we had an old cemetery down the road. Our ancestors were buried there like, Chup Tim-Tim, my grandfather, as well as Daddy's five-year-old sister Bertha, who died from the flu epidemic of 1934.

Down from the cemetery was the Petit family home. Our house, with chipped white paint and warped boards, was surrounded by acres of tall grasses, plots of fragrant mock orange, and a forest filled with chirping squirrels and robins. We had three bedrooms, a living room, a kitchen, a mudroom, and a newly built bathroom with an indoor toilet. Getting a toilet inside was one of the happiest days of my life. When I was little, I dreaded stepping off the back porch to the outhouse before bed. It was too close to the woods! Daddy would have to coax me to go out.

"But Daddy, I'm scared. What about t'siyatkʰu·ʳ?"

I'd peer out into the woods as Daddy grinned.

"Old Sasquatch won't bother you. First, he's shy. Second, he's over six feet tall and smells like a wet dog. And third, well, if he does bother you, you must've been misbehaving."

I wasn't too sure about the shy part.

Regardless, my trips to the outhouse at night were few and far between—and extremely brief.

Daddy's cousin Harlin's house was just a half mile away from us. Cousin Harlin and Daddy were really close. Like brothers close. They talked story all the time, especially about World War II.

"It was right after Pearl Harbor," Daddy began, "when I conned Harlin into joining the navy with me. We both needed to get off the rez before we got into any more trouble with the law." He meant that the way they were going, jail would be their next residence.

According to Cousin Harlin, it was a rainy summer morning when this big bus came barreling down the road.

"It squealed to a stop, splattering mud every-where, right in front of the Grand Ronde Community Center. Then the Indian agent jumped off and said, 'Any man who comes on this bus will be guaranteed three meals a day, clothes on his back, a place to sleep, and a paycheck. All he has to do is get on this bus!'"

"And you got on the bus?" asked Peewee.

"Well, yeah," Cousin Harlin said. "Lots of young guys from the rez took advantage of that deal. John and I were no exception. Hey, we pounced on that bus like a rabbit jumping into a snare."

"After everyone came aboard," Daddy said, "the bus blew off the rez, zipped down Highway 22, and didn't stop until it was in front of an army recruiting station in Salem! But I told Harlin that I didn't want to join the army—you get shot at there. So I convinced him to sign up for the navy. They promised anyone who joined them would see the world."

"Yeah, but they forgot to tell us that the

world was made up of three-fourths water," Cousin Harlin said. Then they both howled, holding their coffee mugs in the air.

After the war, Daddy and Cousin Harlin still did everything together. They both got married and worked for the Long Bell Lumber Company and its mill up in Longview, Washington, on the Columbia River. Daddy sometimes stayed away from home for weeks on end, but he didn't mind. It was a job that paid money. He had a family to support. That was what he cared about.

When Daddy's big frame stomped home on those rare weeks off, he'd brush out wood chips stuck in his buzz-cut black hair. Mama usually had a steaming pot of seasoned deer meat, potatoes, carrots, and onions in salted gravy stirred up on the old woodstove. She'd greet him in the kitchen.

"Dinner will be ready soon," she would say as she checked the biscuits in the oven.

Daddy would take a whiff of the stew and then grab Mama around the waist. "You're the prettiest girl on the rez, and I'm the handsomest guy. How about a smooch?"

She'd shove him off and threaten him with a wooden spoon and a smile.

"Johnny Petit, the girls are watching." Mama didn't care for showing affection in public.

"No, we're not," Peewee would say, giggling from the kitchen table and drawing pictures to decorate the walls.

Mama wasn't an Indian, by the way. She was Portuguese from the Azores. But with dark brown eyes and hair, she didn't stand out. Everyone on the rez called her "the Portuguese Woman," not by her nickname, Cate, and definitely not by her real name, Catarina. If that bothered her, she didn't say so. And for a Portuguese woman, that was pretty hard to do.

Best thing of all was that Chich lived with us. Most Grand Ronde homes had three generations in one house. Each night, Chich combed my long dark hair, saying, "Never cut it. It's a powerful part of your Umpqua identity. When we cut our hair, it shows everyone that we are mourning the death of someone close to us."

That always made me think of Chup. He had lived with us too until his big heart attack. Since the rez doctor only visited the clinic two times a week, Chup died on a day when the doctor wasn't in. He died before our tribe was terminated, so he was still Indian when he was buried.

Chup's funeral was over at St. Michael's Church, with a big giveaway afterward just up the road at the community center. Giveaways help family and others in the community remember a person or an event.

For Chup's giveaway, smoked salmon, homemade breads, and every kind of berry pie covered long tables. Another table held homemade doilies, tablecloths, and extra pies as giveaways. Some elders and those close to Chup received gifts. Everyone in the community gathered at the center and shared a meal. The grown-ups visited while us kids ran around the hall.

From the wake to the burial, there was a lot

of singing. Our voices helped Chup get to the next place, making sure he felt comfortable and stayed there.

There in the hall, as daylight faded, an elder pounded the table with his hand flat. Then he'd pound again. And again. A rhythm sprang from the pounding. A drumbeat. Three poundings, then a pause. Three poundings, then a pause. Soon the other men in their dress slacks, shirts, and ties sat down at the long table and joined in. We kids stopped running around.

Then the elder wailed. "Aaaahhh . . . aiye . . . oooh . . ." The other men joined in, repeating this and singing a song I'd never heard.

I leaned over to Chich, my curiosity piqued. "What are they singing?" I whispered.

"It's an honor song, sweetie, for your chup," Chich said.

"How do they all know the song?"

"They heard it many times before. It's been passed down from family to family."

Daddy leaned over too. "We used to sing this during the day. But now we do it at night."

"Why?" I asked.

"The Indian agent told us to stop. Frightened the next-door neighbors." He leaned even closer. "Thought we might be on the warpath." Then he winked. Daddy seemed to find everything funny.

Later that night, we had a ceremony to burn Chup's clothes and other items not given away. It was a special time.

Our family visited Chup every Sunday after Mass. His old, beat-up logging cap sat atop the cedar board above his grave. Most of the graves had cedar boards covering the plots so family and friends could place items on them that the dead had enjoyed when alive. Chich had placed some cattail dolls on Bertha's board.

Strolling around the cemetery, I would check out all the neat stuff on the graves, like silver thimbles on top of Aunt Ivy's or metal carving tools on top of Uncle Joe's. But there was no taking or removing *anything* from the cemetery. Chich and other elders taught us that anyone who disturbed and disrespected the spirits like that would put themselves at serious risk! I didn't doubt that for a minute.

Things changed at home after Chup died. Chich had her long, silver-streaked hair cut short in a ceremony to mourn Chup. Each chilly grey morning, as she twisted Peewee's and my straight dark hair into two lengthy braids, we missed hearing Chup's stories. After she finished, she would put on her well-loved yellow apron and make us hot, clumpy oatmeal with dried huckleberries and cups of coffee mixed with lots of canned Carnation milk and sugar. Then Peewee and I would head outside to play or head over to the Indian Agency school. Daddy would hitch a ride with Cousin Harlin to the mill while Mama whisked down the road for her waitress job at the rez diner. And Chich, well, she sewed, made pies, and did whatever else grandmothers did.

If I got up early enough, I'd join Chich on the porch to wawa-laxayam·ɾ kitəp-san·ɾ, or greet the day. We'd sit together—she with her coffee and me wrapped in my favorite wool blanket—waiting for the morning sun to reach Spirit Mountain.

"Remember that mountain is sacred to our people," she would say. "It is a good sign if you see saxali-tayi, so pay attention."

I'd keep my eyes peeled. And sometimes I'd see a great bald eagle soar beyond the pines, thankful to call Grand Ronde home, just like me.

3
DIVISIONS

The year I turned eight, I knew change was coming to Grand Ronde. The rez buzzed continuously with reports. Almost every night that winter, our family hustled over to the community center for what were called "informational" meetings hosted by the Indian agent. Even the elders' Friday night bingo was canceled, which almost never happened.

I never understood everything being said. Us kids usually ended up inside the large community pantry playing with old toys or outside on the church's playground with the merry-go-round and swings.

Even when it rained, I preferred to be

outside with my cousins, but that day it was cold. Indians shouted at the white men in suits or at one another. Angry words flew. Threats of battle. I cowered near the pantry window.

"No! We won't leave our homes!" one Indian said.

"We do not want your money!" said another.

"You cannot trust the government!" Chich said.

"They are offering us a better life," said Daddy. His view did not seem to be shared by the others.

Frustration poured from the community room. Indians against the government. Family member against family member. Old against young.

I stared out the window at the soggy playground outside. I felt like this was what the Indian agent must have wanted all along. Us fighting.

At home, I asked Daddy what the meetings were about. Why was everyone so angry?

"The government just doesn't want to be in

the Indian business anymore," he said, leaning back in his chair.

Mama said, "Someone from the Bureau of Indian Affairs had the nerve to say, 'Cate, you might as well get used to it.'" Then she struck a match to light her second cigarette with the first one still burning in the ashtray.

The Bureau of Indian Affairs, or the BIA for short, was the government agency that sent those white men in suits to tell us Grand Ronders we were about to be terminated.

Our old schoolhouse had just been painted a new coat of yellow. You would think if the government painted it, they were planning on keeping it. I didn't understand what they wanted with all our old buildings anyway. I worried about Chup.

"What about our cemetery?" I asked, looking over at Chich.

"They have promised to not take our cemetery from us," she said. I didn't know if I believed it. But maybe the government couldn't sell a graveyard anyway.

The fighting at the community center didn't

change anything. Our tribe was against termination, but the BIA superintendent lied and said we
were for it, claiming we took a vote. But no vote
was ever taken in Grand Ronde.

But I didn't know any of this had happened.
Spring came, then summer and my birthday. I
was starting to think we would be left alone. But
we weren't.

4
THE OREGONIAN

Summer had been full of fun times, me celebrating my eighth birthday and playing with my cousins and friends. Then one late August afternoon, I decided to race home from Cousin Harlin's house to give Chich a new picture I'd drawn for our farmhouse walls. Cutting through the wild barley, I sprinted past his older boys, Mark and Chip, playing out in the field. With my waist-long braids soaring behind me, I almost made it past Peewee and Leroy, Cousin Harlin's youngest boy, when Leroy pushed her toward me. Peewee punched Leroy hard in the shoulder while I zigzagged to the side, leaving them behind.

"Hey Regina!" Leroy yelled as he grabbed his shoulder. "Where ya going so fast?"

"Home!" I responded. Didn't glance back. Just kept on going.

I bolted inside the house, calling for Chich, ready to show her my drawing. The front door slammed against the wall, something never allowed. I was almost into the next room before I noticed there'd been no reply. I stopped. And listened.

"Chich?"

A quiet sob whispered from the kitchen. I crept into the room, hugging my arms and picture tight to my brown plaid dress. The drawn kitchen curtains blocked most of the sunlight.

Chich sat at the scarred breakfast table, her wrinkled brown hands trembling, holding *The Oregonian* newspaper.

I had never seen Chich cry before. I held my breath. *Somebody must have died*, I thought. Could it be an accident at Daddy's logging camp? It wasn't uncommon for people to get hurt with chainsaws and fir trees crashing down.

 19

I finally breathed. "What's wrong?"

Chich looked up from the paper, her eyes red. Mine began to fill. "The president has just signed a bill from Congress saying that we're no longer Indian," Chich said as she wiped her eyes with a dishrag.

"We're no longer Indian?" I dropped my prized drawing. My mind raced, trying to understand. All I could say was, "But . . . but what if I still want to be one?"

I felt devastated when Daddy came home and confirmed what the newspaper said. According to *The Oregonian*, it was the law. Public Law 588, to be exact. Signed by President Eisenhower on August 13, 1954, the law said the government didn't need to provide for our education, health care, or anything else as promised in the treaties. The government declared us only Americans now instead of our own nation. We didn't need a reservation anymore. Nor our tribal roll numbers. Really?

The article said that many other Indian tribes had been terminated in Oregon, and it had been happening to other tribes elsewhere within the

United States. Mama bawled, covering her face with her flowered handkerchief. Chich wiped away angry tears. Peewee and I nibbled on dry cornflakes at the table, as quietly as possible. Best not to ask questions when adults were upset.

"Well, it's done," Daddy said, sipping his coffee and staring out the kitchen window.

Mama flailed. "What are we going to do?" She paced the kitchen. "Where are we going to go?"

"tənəs-man, you are Indian," Chich said to Daddy while stroking my hair. "I am Indian. The girls are Indians. Fight this." She looked at me. "For them."

Daddy leaned forward. "With what? Good looks? I know I'm handsome and all, but you know we can't fight the government." He stood up, facing us. "It will all work out in the end. Trust me. I'll take care of us."

And then Daddy took it upon himself to change our lives forever.

5

SOUTHBOUND

Daddy had plans, all right.

In the late spring of 1957, Daddy signed us up for the federal government's Indian Relocation Program. The government promised Indians a better home, furniture, schooling, and a good job. Daddy called it an *opportunity* and seemed to believe it. Chich called it an eviction.

The termination law said we could buy our land if we wanted to stay, but we couldn't afford it. Almost no Grand Ronder could. The government marked up the land prices two to three times what the lots would normally sell for. Everybody on the rez said no one should pay that much, even if they could. Some families who could afford it put their money together to buy their allotments or bought cheaper land nearby. This wasn't an option for us, but we held on as long as we could until we were forced to move.

When Daddy announced we'd be leaving for Los Angeles, California, in July, Mama sobbed for three days and smoked a whole carton of Pall Malls. She got a headache so fierce she threw up. This didn't help her hundred-pound body weight.

"I've never lived outside our reservation," I said, sketching on a piece of paper Mama had given me to keep me busy while she packed. "What if I can't be Indian in Los Angeles?"

"Of course you'll be Indian," Mama said, carefully folding my clothes into a battered suitcase she got from someone at the diner. "You'll just be living differently."

I scribbled hard, digging my pencil deeper into the paper and causing the lead to break. "What will it be like?" I asked.

"It will be like here, only different," Mama said.

I slumped over my drawing. "Geez! That's no answer."

Daddy poked his head through my bedroom door. "What's no answer?"

"Mama says living in the city is the same as living here but different." I rolled my eyes. "What kind of answer is that?"

"Hey, watch how you talk to your mama," Daddy said, sitting on my bed. "Look at it this way. The city has houses, yards, schools, stores just like Grand Ronde. They just have more of them and more people." He gave me a hug. "But we won't know how it is living there until we get there, right?"

"But what if we don't like living there?" I looked at Mama. "Can we move back home?"

Mama glanced at Daddy. Then she continued packing.

Daddy smiled. "Sure. But first we need to give Los Angeles a chance. When I was traveling in the navy, and even now being away logging, I saw more jobs in other towns. I know I can get a better job down in California with more pay and not be gone from my girls all the time."

I couldn't say I really believed him after

listening to the other adults in the community. To them, we were about to be cheated, just like we always had been by the government.

The summer morning we left, a misty fog covered the train station so thick that the morning sun struggled to peek through. A few family members stood around saying good-bye. Chich spoke in Chinuk Wawa to Aunt Rosie, her younger sister and Cousin Harlin's mama. I considered it their secret language. When adults didn't want us kids to know what was going on, they usually spoke it.

Chich smoothed away strands of black hair, sprinkled with gray, from her sister's tearstained face and then adjusted her straw hat. Aunt Rosie pulled out a handkerchief from her overstuffed pocketbook. Wiped her eyes. Blew her nose.

Meanwhile Mama busied herself by fussing over Peewee and me. "Quit fidgeting with your dresses," she said. "We need to look our best for the trip."

Peewee and I wore matching store-bought crinoline dresses but in different colors. Mine was blue. Peewee's was pink. I didn't care much for them. The fabric scratched so bad it was like hornets biting my legs. My black-and-white saddle shoes blistered my heels. But I was stuck with this outfit, instead of the wonderful handmade dresses Chich sewed for us each year.

"You know, you can't trust the government," Cousin Harlin kept saying, smashing a cigarette against the sole of his boot. "Remember what the elders have told us." Cousin Harlin and his family weren't coming with us. This would be the first time he didn't follow Daddy.

"Well, I can't stay here," Daddy replied. "And you know how I hate working at the mill. I'm better than that."

"You are Indian, right?" Cousin Harlin said. They both chuckled. "You think the government will really find you a better job?"

"Hey, the government and the navy are the same. You get jobs you're qualified for. Same pay. Same work. Move up in rank."

"Yeah. Go from scrubbing latrines to scraping paint off a ship. I remember." Cousin Harlin grabbed hold of Daddy's shoulder. "You better hope those government men keep those promises, or you're going to end up without a canoe to get back home." Then they both chuckled and hugged.

The train arrived. The conductor shouted for us to climb aboard. More tears. Big hugs. Daddy carried our bigger suitcase and Chich's portable Singer sewing machine onboard while Mama toted the medium-sized bag.

The long train slowly cut across the land throughout the day and then accelerated into the night. The train's wheels pounded the tracks, like beating a log drum. Windows shook like dance rattles. I looked outside. Darkness looked back.

Chich stared out the window too, her hands folded on top of her navy-blue clutch bag. I scooted right next to her. Peewee leaned in from the other side. Chich wrapped her arms around us and looked down. "You better go to sleep," she said. "Morning comes early."

"I can't sleep," Peewee said, yawning. "Could you maybe tell us a story?"

"What kind of story?"

"A good story," Peewee answered.

"Mmm, a good story, huh?"

Now stories from Chich weren't exactly the "Once upon a time" or "They lived happily ever after" stories. Indian stories spoke truth. Well, that was what Chich said.

Then she began:

Before Grand Ronde became a reservation, our people, the Umpquas, lived down south in our plankhouses on our farms. We had lived this way for as long as we could remember. But white settlers demanded more land. So in the winter of 1856, the Indian agent came to our people and said they had to move to Grand Ronde, a reservation some one hundred and fifty miles away. Forced to leave their homes, our ancestors left only with the clothes on their backs and what little they could carry.

Other tribes from around the area were rounded up too and joined our people on the journey north. But none of those tribes wanted to leave their homes.

They walked through mud, rain, and snow. Men. Women. Children. Elders.

The Indian agent only had eight wagons to carry those who couldn't walk, which was not enough. Five Indians, including children, died because of the harsh conditions, and one was murdered.

At the end of the journey, federal soldiers corralled our ancestors and those of more than thirty other tribes to our home in Grand Ronde. None of those people ever got money for all that they left behind—their houses, crops, beads, tools, horses, canoes, and dentalium shells.

My chich was six years old when she walked that trail. She remembered soldiers shouting for them to keep moving. And she remembered her chich dying one night on the journey when the group stopped to camp. They quickly buried her without any of the proper ceremonies.

"I would never do that to you, Chich." I hugged her.

"Neither would I." Peewee hugged her too.

Chich smiled and hugged us back. "I know. But children often don't have choices."

Peewee wiped away a tear. "That's a sad story, Chich."

"It can be seen as a sad story," Chich agreed. "But it is also a proud story. Many more tribes were removed and brought to Grand Ronde to form our community. The story shows that our people survive. Even in the harshest conditions."

"Then you think we will survive this move?" I asked.

Chich looked out the window, pursing her lips. Then she stroked our hair. "Well, we are Umpquas. And we come from survivors. What do *you* think?"

Like I said, our stories strike a different chord than fairytales.

Morning came, changing midnight skies into robin's-egg blue. I stared out the window from the passenger car. Tall poles held thick black wires that waved across the rows of crowded business buildings. Ford Fairlanes and Chevrolet Bel Airs whizzed by along the highways and paved city streets. I saw nothing with green firs or black cottonwoods. No golden-yellow fields. No silvery-white streams. No emerald-green mountains.

No familiar homeland at all.

6

COURTESY OF THE GOVERNMENT

Our family arrived in Los Angeles on July 9, 1957. The train station was huge compared to the tiny one we'd left in Salem. Rows upon rows of polished wooden benches lined the floor. A gigantic clock hung high above the front doors. Speakers blasted times and places. People rushed by, whipping around us. Some even pushed us aside. No one spoke to us or seemed to notice we were there.

"Time to track down this Indian agent," Daddy said, wiping the sweat from his brow and hooking his black jacket over his arm. "He should have been here to meet us."

We walked out of the station into the dry,

hot air. This didn't feel like home at all.

Daddy set our big suitcase and Chich's sewing machine down on the curb. He pulled a piece of paper from his wallet. A white man wearing a tie and a short-sleeved shirt hurried toward us. "Are you the Petit family?"

"Yes, we've been waiting for you," Daddy replied.

"I apologize. I'm Steve Parsons with the Bureau of Indian Affairs. Parked right over here." He carried the smaller of our two suitcases and Chich's sewing machine to his car while Daddy lugged the bigger suitcase. After Mr. Parsons set our things by the trunk and opened the passenger side back door, Mama, Chich, Peewee, and I climbed into the back seat. Daddy loaded in our bags and slid into the front seat next to the agent.

As we headed away from the station, Peewee and I craned our necks to see out of the front and side windows.

"What's that?!" I asked as what looked like a large metal box slid to a stop ahead of us.

"That's a streetcar. It's like a little train in

the city that moves people around," Mr. Parsons replied.

Wow, a streetcar, so many buildings, so many people. Everywhere I looked was filled with something or someone.

Soon we moved out of taller buildings to an area with diners, shops, and little houses.

"Hey, how about we stop at that Chinese restaurant I see up there on the right? Grab some dinner to go. You girls have to try it. I haven't had any since I was in the navy," said Daddy.

We waited in the car while Daddy and Mr. Parsons went in and ordered our dinner. I didn't know what kind of food came from a Chinese restaurant, but really nothing I had seen here yet looked familiar.

I crinkled up my nose when they returned. Chinese food didn't smell like venison stew.

When we pulled up in front of the house on 58th Place, no one said anything. Mr. Parsons helped Daddy with our suitcases as we scooted out of the backseat.

Our old wooden farmhouse had plenty of land

to live, play, and explore. But this little stucco box? Well, it rested on six feet of front yard, eight feet of backyard, and a yardstick of dirt between the houses.

"These houses are so close together, you can taste your neighbor's pot roast from your window," Mama said as she walked up the porch steps to the front door.

I stared at the surroundings. Busy asphalt streets replaced isolated dirt roads. Concrete replaced grass. In fact, there was a concrete path that stretched from our concrete porch to the concrete sidewalk.

"Not many plants to speak of," Chich said.

Mr. Parsons didn't offer to show us around. He just gave Daddy the keys and then had him sign some papers on the car hood. He handed Daddy a catalog with some classes Daddy would need to enroll in for next month. Then Mr. Parsons wished us luck and drove off.

Inside, the house was furnished, courtesy of the government, and it wasn't much better. Peewee sat on the faded couch. I walked into the kitchen with Mama to inspect a greasy gas stove and a refrigerator that smelled like sour milk. Chich sat down in one of the rusty mint-green chairs that matched the metal kitchen table.

"Hey, there's a washing machine in here," Daddy said as he glanced in the small room just past the kitchen. He put our suitcases in our rooms and Peewee and I explored the rest of the house. There were two twin beds in one bedroom and one bigger bed in the other with a bathroom in between.

Daddy plopped down the sacks full of white paper cartons from the Chinese restaurant. Sweet-and-sour shrimp, chow mein, egg rolls, fried and white rice, and five cans of pop covered the table.

"Not crazy about chow mein tonight, girls?" Daddy asked as Peewee and I looked at the food we'd never seen before. We decided to try some white rice and a piece of shrimp without the sauce. "Come on, Cate, isn't this great? Look. We have a gas stove now instead of an old wood stove."

Mama wouldn't respond. Daddy tried again to be positive.

"Trust me," he said, taking her hand. "It will all work out. Next month, I'll be in electronics school. I'll have a great job by December."

Mama jumped out of her chair. "You think this is great? We left our home to live in this *dump*!" Her lips quivered. Tears formed in her eyes.

"Don't cry, Mama," Peewee said, patting her hand. "It's not that bad."

Mama sat back down and touched Peewee's hair.

Daddy stood up, folding his arms across his puffed-up chest and then stretching them out wide, smiling. "Coming . . . here . . . makes . . . us . . . Americans," he said, imitating Burt Lancaster in that *Apache* movie he and Cousin Harlin had seen when they worked up at that mill near Portland. "Soon . . . we be white people. Living in good house. Working good job. Getting good life." His gray eyes twinkled. "Indian no more."

He pulled Mama to him. "Come, woman. Give me a smooch."

Mama struggled hard not to smile. "John, stop it. The girls are here," she said.

Peewee and I laughed and immediately came to her rescue, tugging her away from Daddy's grip.

Chich kept quiet as she cleared the table, cleaned off the dishes, and put them away in the cupboard. "I'm going to bed now," she said. "Good night."

That night, sharing one of the twin beds with Peewee, I listened to the sounds in our new home. I heard every car that drove by, every breath from Mama and Daddy in the next room. But Chich's muffled sobs from the other twin bed made my eyes wet.

I prayed to saxali-tayi that Daddy would take us home. That he would come to his senses, as Chich said, and see we didn't belong here.

But that did not happen.

7
MEETING THE NEIGHBORS

Even though that tiny stucco house wasn't anything like our rez home, it did have one feature I loved. From the living room, I could race through our bedroom into the bathroom, over to Mama's and Daddy's bedroom, then through the kitchen and back out into the living room—one giant circle. Trust me, I couldn't do that in the old farmhouse. Peewee and I kept chasing each other around and around until Chich stretched her arm out.

"You two sound like a pair of wild raccoons," she said, propping the broom against our bedroom wall. "Go play outside. It's beautiful this morning." She grabbed two cattail dolls she had made before leaving Grand Ronde and held them out to us.

Peewee and I took the dolls and ran out into the front yard. There we scavenged for sticks and leaves to make tiny lean-tos, the summer homes some Indians make when they're away from home fishing, hunting, and gathering. Back on the rez, Daddy taught us how to make them one Saturday afternoon while Mama waited tables at the diner and Chich visited Aunt Rosie.

As we constructed our lean-tos, the sun blazed above. The traffic noise from Western Avenue rumbled over to our street. I glanced up, checking out the neighborhood. That's when I noticed a boy on the sidewalk staring at Peewee and me.

His white T-shirt and tan shorts accented his skinny black frame. He said nothing. Just stared. Standing next to him was his younger sister, I assumed, with four ponytail braids all held closed at the ends with different colorful barrettes.

I was startled at first, wondering why they didn't say hello or something to let us know they were there.

As I stood and dusted the dry grass from my knees, the girl blurted out, "Are you Indians? Our parents said Indians were moving in."

"Yeaaah," I said slowly as I studied these new kids. They didn't look like any of the kids back in Grand Ronde. I'd never seen anyone so dark. "We're Umpqua. What are you?"

The boy looked at me as if I had sprouted antlers. "We're *colored*," the boy answered.

Now I was really confused. "What do you mean *colored*?"

"We're *Negroes*," the girl added.

I had never heard of that one. "Okay. What tribe is that?"

The boy's mouth dropped open, and he burst out laughing, like I had asked a dumb question. The girl giggled so hard, she snorted.

"We're not from an Indian tribe. Don't think there're any tribes in Arkansas where we moved from, just white folks that don't want us around," the boy finally said. "Haven't you ever met Negroes before?"

"No," I huffed.

"Nope, you're the first ones ever," Peewee chimed in with a smile, holding out both our dolls. "Wanna play?"

That Peewee. She made friends everywhere.

"Is this a real Indian doll?" the girl asked, checking out Peewee's cattail doll.

"Our chich made it, so I guess it is." Peewee grinned.

"Chich?" asked the boy.

"That's how we say grandmother," I said.

The girl studied the doll. She then squatted down to check out our lean-tos. She looked puzzled by the mass of tiny leaves, flowers, and twigs. "Is this how you live back where you came from?"

"No," Peewee replied. "We had a house back home. This is a lean-to."

I whispered to the boy, "Does she always ask so many questions?"

"Yep. 'Nosy' is what we call her at home."

The girl jumped up from the grass and bolted up the porch steps. "My name's Addie

Bates and he's Keith," she declared. "Can we see your house?"

Peewee and I gave each other a sidelong glance. "Sure," Peewee said. "I'm Theresa, but everyone calls me Peewee, and she's Regina."

"Where are your Indian blankets?" Addie asked as Keith and I entered the house behind them. "And how come your couch has stains?"

I cringed. I hadn't thought about how bad the couch looked.

"Chich crochets all our blankets," Peewee said. "And the government gave us this couch."

"The government gave you a couch?" Addie asked.

"Yeah," I said. "They gave us all this furniture. Well, except for Chich's sewing machine. We brought that from the rez."

"The rez?"

"Our Indian reservation," I replied.

"What's that?"

"It's land where Indians live, work, and go to school. Ours is in Oregon," I said, wondering if I was lying because it didn't exist anymore after being terminated.

"And you guys know how to sew?" Addie continued.

"Addie," Keith said, pulling on the back of his sister's blouse, "shut up."

Addie scrunched up her face. "Ooh. You told me to shut up. I'm going to tell Mama."

We continued the tour and entered the kitchen. Mama was scrubbing out the refrigerator, stopping only long enough to take a drag from her cigarette. She acknowledged us with a nod. The scent of vinegar filled the air.

From the kitchen, we headed out back. Chich was there, supervising Daddy putting up the clothesline. He stretched the rope from the back porch onto the small garage as tight as he could.

"Chich, this is Keith and Addie," I said.

Chich smiled at them, and Daddy walked over to us. His large frame towered over our new friends. They stepped back to give him room.

"Does this work for you, Ma?" Daddy asked Chich, pointing to the clothesline.

"It'll do," she said, nodding. She turned to us. "How about I make some sandwiches for you all?" Without waiting for an answer, she headed inside.

Daddy surveyed Keith and Addie and smiled. "You live close by?"

"Yes sir," Keith said. "We live across the street and two houses down from you."

"Nice to meet you. Why don't you kids head back in for those sandwiches?" Daddy started putting his tools away.

We raced back inside. While we nibbled on peanut butter sandwiches at the kitchen table, Mama went to arrange stuff in the bathroom. Addie told us all kinds of stories about the neighborhood and the kids on the street—kids we had yet to meet.

Hanging out with Keith and Addie felt kind of like spending time with my cousins back home. So that's why I couldn't have guessed what was coming next.

8

THE WRONG KIND OF INDIANS

Addie ran home to get some pink plastic dolls and doll beds, and Keith brought back toy bows and arrows, decorated with brightly-colored feathers and fake leather.

"Can you teach me how you shoot an arrow?" Keith asked, handing me the bow.

"I don't know how to shoot," I said, and handed it back.

"Doesn't your daddy own a bow and arrow?"

My brow wrinkled. "I don't think so." I looked over at Peewee sitting with Addie, who was going nonstop with questions.

"What about an Indian costume?" Addie asked her.

"Costume? No. Why would I wear a costume?" Peewee seemed perplexed. Frankly, I was too.

Addie threw her hands in the air. "Geez, what kind of Indians are you? Do you even have a tipi?"

I never thought about it. Tipis, Indian costumes. Heck, I never saw tipis or any of that stuff, except in a couple of old cowboy comic books at Cousin Harlin's house.

I realized that unless we did something Indian, these new friends wouldn't believe we were. And I wasn't about to let them think that. "I bet Daddy knows how to make one. He can make anything!"

I raced inside the house and found Daddy relaxed on the couch, reading the *Los Angeles Examiner*. "Keith and Addie are asking us to make a tipi. Do you know how to make one?"

Daddy furrowed his black eyebrows and put down his paper. "What?" he asked.

I repeated the question.

"Umpqua don't have tipis," he said. "Just make them a lean-to like I taught you."

"But they don't want a lean-to. They want a tipi. That's what Indians make."

Daddy laughed. "Well, not an Umpqua Indian. You know that."

He went back to reading his paper. I sighed.

Meanwhile, Peewee poked her head in the door. She signaled me to follow her outside. "Keith said he would make one."

"A tipi?!"

She nodded. "He went home to get supplies."

A little later, Keith showed up in the backyard with some rope, an old bedsheet, some long nails, and a hammer. He walked over to the young walnut tree that stood near our tall wooden fence. He studied the tree. Then he tied the top part of the sheet around the tree trunk with rope.

"Where did you learn that?" I finally asked, watching how he knotted the rope in ways I had never seen before.

"Boy Scouts," Keith said. From there he stretched the sheet outward and nailed the edges to the ground. The entrance was one flap of the sheet that hung inside the tipi. "So, what do you think?" he asked me, his chest sticking out.

I raised my eyebrows. "Well, it's much better than what I would have made." I didn't know what Boy Scouts were, but there was a lot I didn't know about life outside Grand Ronde.

Peewee and I used that tipi with our friends all afternoon. And the day after that. And the day after that. More questions were asked in that tipi than I had ever heard before.

9
PLANKHOUSE PEOPLE

With all these questions and talk about "real" Indians, I knew who would have the answers. Chich.

"How come our people don't make tipis?" I asked that night while we were getting ready for bed. I sat on Peewee's and my bed, taking down my braids so Chich could brush my hair as she did each night.

"Because our people didn't move around like Plains Indians," she said. "We built plankhouses from wood, fished in the rivers, and cultivated camas and other crops."

"But Addie said all Indians make tipis."

"Oh, is that so?" Chich said, eyebrow raised.

She tucked Peewee in her side of the bed and kissed her cheek. She then sat on my side to brush my hair.

I was deep in thought. Back home we didn't have to prove we were Indian. Everyone on the rez knew. Even the white people who lived there knew. No one ever showed up in headdresses or buckskins or carried around bows and arrows. But in the city, I guess Indians had to show, not tell.

Chich seemed to read my mind. "Some people think Indians still live like they did before the white man came."

"Back then we had headdresses and bows and arrows?" asked Peewee.

"No," Chich replied, gently working the knots out of the ends of my hair.

"How come you don't have an Indian costume?" I asked her. "Addie says we're not Indians unless we have costumes."

"It seems Addie thinks she knows more about us being Indians than we do," Chich said. She tucked me in, kissed my cheek, and sat over on her bed. We listened.

I remember my mama owning a traditional dress, but it wasn't a costume. It was beautiful. I asked her once why she didn't wear it anymore. She told me how when she was little, the Indian agent would gather our people up in their deerskin regalia adorned with shells and parade them through town like circus acts. She didn't like the white folks' stares.

Then onlookers from the town would follow our people back to the rez, expecting a show. And the Indian agent would have them perform for the crowd. They danced. And sang. And drummed, while the Indian agent collected money for himself. Because of that, many stopped wearing their regalia.

A person gets tired of being treated like a circus animal.

Chich coughed a couple of times and pressed her hand to her chest.

"Are you all right, Chich?" I jumped up and placed my hand on hers. "Do you need your pill?"

The doctor back on the rez had given Chich some pills for her heart, which didn't beat like it should. Seeing her hand on her heart like that made mine hurt, too.

"I'm fine. It's nothing. Just my heart fluttering." She smiled. "Now, where was I?"

"Our people danced for the townsfolk," said Peewee.

"That's right."

And with that, Chich let me tuck the covers up around her.

"I don't think Addie and Keith will believe we're really Indian unless we have something that shows we're Indian," I said.

"Regina, just remember this. You were born an Indian. Peewee is Indian. It's our Umpqua stories and traditions that keep you Indian. You don't need to dress up to prove that." Chich gave a tired smile and then turned over, facing the wall.

I sighed. Knowing you were Indian was one thing. Proving it was quite another.

10

BOWS, ARROWS & TV INDIANS

Peewee didn't mind Addie's constant questions or opinions about everything. But then, Peewee was more easygoing and loved to have lots of friends. Keith was quieter. With him I usually had to start the conversation. We sat outside, sipping Kool-Aid. After talking with Chich last night, I had some questions of my own.

"Why do you think my family should have things like tipis and costumes?" I asked.

"Well, because that's what Indians have. I saw it on TV," he said. "You guys live on a lot of land, hunt wild things, and have fun."

"Yeah. It's fun living on the rez. I can see

Spirit Mountain, all kinds of trees, and my relatives' houses nearby. All of Daddy's cousins get together with their shotguns and hunt deer. While they're gone, the women make the breads and pies. They have us kids cut up the vegetables for the stew."

The memory of our deer hunts made me sad for Grand Ronde. The hunters would ask for saxali-tayi's help in providing food for their families and the community. When the men came home, the deer would be hung up and slaughtered. They took time to thank the deer for giving up their lives for us.

After they processed the meat, the men would distribute portions throughout their families. The women marinated the meat in spices, then fried it or placed it inside a big pot of stew. Sometimes it seemed like forever before the food was served. But when it was, everyone ate to their heart's content.

Now none of that was going to happen on 58th Place.

"No bows and arrows?" Keith asked.

I laughed. "You could use bows and arrows, but my daddy and his cousins don't."

"But in the movies . . . ."

I smirked. "How about your people?" I asked Keith. "Do they hunt?"

Keith's eyes widened. "Are you kidding? We always lived in the city. We buy our meat at the store. In fact, that's where we buy all our food." He paused. "Do you even have grocery stores?"

"Yes. You sure seem to think we live like those Indians you watch on TV."

I watched Keith sip his Kool-Aid. He seemed in deep thought, like he wanted to say something but didn't. So I asked him, "What do your people look like on TV? Does it show how they lived long ago?"

"Only if you watch Tarzan movies. We wear loincloths, carry spears, and do a lot of mumbling. And it seems like we're scared of every animal around."

"That sounds weird. I never saw any of those movies. People think you're like that?"

"I don't know. But whites and sometimes other folks do see us as different."

Different. That was how I was feeling since moving to LA.

11

SUMMER IN THE CITY

Figuring out how to be an Indian in the city with no cousins to play with wasn't easy. I missed our adventures through the woods, creeks and fields back home. At least Peewee and I had our new friends, Addie and Keith. And they were about to introduce us to a couple of other kids on our street—Anthony and Philip.

Clear skies and a full sun met us out in the street. We walked toward the corner of Western Avenue and 58th Place. Keith and Addie led the way. "Anthony and Philip live there," Keith said, pointing to a square white house at the end of the block. "They moved here before we did.

Their last name is Hernández. They're Cuban."

We wandered into the brothers' front yard with rows of kitchen chairs, benches, stools and a few milk crates lined up in front of a professional-looking puppet theater stand. The sun spot-lighted a tall box carved out of dark wood with intricate gold-paint designs all around. The arid wind blew at the red velvet curtains and silky tassels.

"'Cuban' isn't a tribe either, I take it," I said.

"Nah, Cuba is an island far away," Keith said. "They speak Spanish there and make cigars."

Addie jumped in. "Anthony says he misses Cuba a lot, especially his cousins."

I understood. I missed mine too.

"And Philip says they can never go back home," she added.

I was about to ask why but then realized I probably knew the answer. If it was anything like what happened to us in Grand Ronde, I knew exactly how Anthony felt.

"They put on good shows," Addie said,

looking for a row of empty seats. "They do this every summer. They've done a magic show, a circus, and a musical."

Anthony, the younger brother, met us and held out his hand to collect admission. "A penny each, please."

The two pennies I received from Chich that morning for Peewee and me clinked in Anthony's hand on top of Keith's money.

Most of the neighborhood kids sat around us. I sat down next to Peewee, who'd sat next to Addie. "Anthony and Philip aren't their real names," Addie said.

"They're not?" I asked.

"They changed them to make it easier for the teachers to say in school," Keith explained, sitting down next to me.

"The government made our elders change their names too. The Indian agent couldn't say them right," I said.

"What were your real names?" asked Keith.

"Don't know. It's been since before Chich was born, maybe even her parents, since anyone said them." I watched Philip and Anthony bring out paper cups through the front door.

"So they gave you 'Petit' as your last name?" Addie asked.

Peewee nodded.

"You know, Petit isn't an American name," Keith said.

I shrugged. I didn't know what it was, except not an Umpqua name.

Mrs. Hernández, wearing a nurse's uniform, brought out small brown paper bags full of fresh, hot popcorn for everyone in the audience.

"Mrs. Hernández was a doctor in Cuba. A real good doctor too," Addie whispered, continuing her gossip. "She's not allowed to doctor here, though."

"Why not?" Peewee asked.

"Mama says it's because she's a Cuban doctor, not an American doctor. Now she's a nurse. But she still helps everyone on our street."

That didn't seem right. Doctors were doctors. Period.

I noticed some white kids filling in the seats.

While Philip offered cups and Anthony poured fruit punch, Mrs. Hernández passed out the popcorn. She stopped in front of Peewee and me.

"¡Hola! ¿Hablan español?"

I leaned back, startled as I took the bag. I'd never heard that language before and didn't know what to say. Peewee's brow scrunched up. "Thank you?" I said, hoping that was the right response.

Mrs. Hernández tilted her head, looking at me. "Oh, I'm sorry," she said, switching to English. "I thought you knew Spanish." She continued giving away popcorn to the rest of the kids.

I looked at Keith. He shrugged. "I don't know what she said either," he offered.

"Do I look like someone who knows Spanish?"

"Well, if I didn't know you were Indian, I would say you look Mexican and they speak Spanish. California used to be part of Mexico. Then the US and Mexico fought a war, and now it's part of the United States."

I nodded like I understood what he was saying. I wondered how many different kinds of people I'd end up meeting in Los Angeles.

When everyone finally settled in, the brothers walked behind the theater. Soon the curtains opened. We applauded when the first marionette, a tall Spanish dancer, came onstage. Her beautiful black lace and red silk attire blew in the breeze. She had long eyelashes and full red lips. As the boys sang, she danced with her wooden high heels clicking. I didn't understand the song, but I liked the melody and rhythm. The puppet twirled and kicked her leg high. She finished with a split, arms in the air. We applauded again. She bowed and left the stage.

The second performance didn't work as smoothly as the first. They brought out a big black bull with giant horns. He pranced around the stage, pawing the floor. His large bulk filled the tiny stage. The bull tripped, dangling off the stage. At one point, he ended up with his behind in the air. Everyone howled with laughter.

When the bull finally straightened himself out, a small man appeared that Keith told me was called a matador. His outfit was adorned with elaborate trim, black cording, and gold buttons. He held a bright red cape in his tiny hands.

He waved his cape, and the audience laughed. The matador was facing the bull's behind. Philip grinned and then twisted the handle to turn the bull around.

Now facing the matador, the bull lowered his head and charged. The matador flew up and disappeared offstage.

The bull looked around, trotting from one end of the stage to the other. When the matador reappeared, he held a tiny sword in one hand. The matador raised his sword at the bull and faced the audience.

He struck the bull on the head with the sword. The bull shook his head and collapsed, his wooden body crashing on the stage. The matador had knocked the bull out. The audience cheered and applauded. Anthony and Philip came out from behind the theater and took a bow.

Afterward, we all helped the brothers put away everything from the yard. When we were all done, Anthony and Philip began suggesting games we could play outside. Playing inside someone's house was never an option—even on a hot day.

"How about war?" Philip said, sitting on the edge of his porch. Carl and Debbie also joined us. Debbie lived across the street and Carl lived next door to the brothers. They seemed a little younger than me and Keith. Carl was white, but I couldn't tell about Debbie. Her hair was light brown and curly, but she actually looked a little like me and Peewee.

"Nah, we played that last time," said Carl. He picked up an empty paper bag, wadded it up like a ball, and threw it at Anthony. "How about baseball?"

"My mom grounded me for a week after we used her couch cushions for bases," Debbie said. "No way."

"I know something way more fun than that," Addie offered. "Regina and Peewee have a tipi in their backyard. We could play Cowboys and Indians."

"Great!" Anthony exclaimed. "We've never had a tipi to play in."

Keith checked over the tipi in the backyard and gave it a thumbs-up. We constructed a soldiers' fort on our front porch using the metal rocker, a card table from Keith's house, and a couple of blankets spread over the top. The teams could run around one end of the house to the other as well as anywhere on the block between our three families' houses. The prisoners either ended up on our porch at the fort or around back inside our tipi.

With everything set up, Philip made all the rules. "The soldiers have the guns, and the Indians have bows and arrows," he declared.

I immediately balked. "Indians have guns, you know," I said. "We play Cowboys and Indians back home too, and all our Indians have guns."

"Indians can't have guns because Indians can't win," Philip responded.

"What?" I stepped back, hands on my hips. "Indians can't have guns because they are automatically supposed to lose the game?!"

"Come on, Philip," Keith said, seeing my expression. My face was getting hotter by the minute. "We're playing with real Indians now. Let them have guns."

"No, that's not how it works," said Philip.

I stood with my arms folded. Six kids stared at me, including Peewee. Apparently, nobody was going to stand up to Philip.

"Come on, Regina," Peewee pleaded. "Let's just play it their way." She didn't care if we had guns or not. She just liked playing.

After some awkward silence, I reluctantly agreed. The Indians would have bows and arrows instead of guns.

The game began. Everyone yelled, running around shooting whatever we had. Sticks. Fake rifles. Plastic bows and arrows. Soon I was captured and stuck on the front porch. I didn't really care to play anymore anyway. At least Peewee was happy.

I sat down with my head on my knees. The game was so much better with our cousins and the bigger kids back in Grand Ronde.

Back home.

12

A DIFFERENT STYLE OF COWBOYS & INDIANS

When we played Cowboys and Indians on the rez, we made sure the Indians had guns and that they could win.

One year, we waited most of the summer until the rains ended to sneak onto Yamhill field, part of Old Man Jenkins's property. Jenkins was white and didn't like what he called "savages" on his land, so we always snuck in. We played right where the field met the tree line.

Skipper and some of the older kids from school brought a bunch of lumber, nails, and hammers and started building a makeshift fort by the tree line. Cousin Harlin's boys, Leroy, Mark, and Chip, followed along with Peewee and me.

"We want to play too," Leroy said.

"Then make your own fort," Skipper said.

We constructed lean-tos from branches on the forest floor.

With everything built, we then divided into two groups. The Indians were the older kids, and the cowboys were us younger ones. Different-sized sticks became horses, bows, and rifles. Skipper outlined the story: Indians were minding their own business when some cowboys came to take over.

"You must leave," said Leroy, aiming his big stick "rifle" at the Indians.

"Nope," said Skipper. "Not gonna happen."

And then the fighting began.

"I shot you! You're dead!"

"No, I'm not! It's just a flesh wound!"

"Hey, watch your stick! It almost hit me in the eye!"

And on it went. The yelping. The hollering. The laughing. The *bang! bang!* of rifles. The *thwish-woosh-thunk* of bows launching imaginary arrows and hitting the cowboys. The "horses" ran around the forts and lean-tos.

Finally, after everyone tired out, Skipper and his gang of Indians declared victory. Everyone jumped up and down, waving sticks in the air, yelling.

Skipper suddenly raised his hand. We all stopped.

"What?" Leroy asked. Skipper motioned to some trees nearby.

One-Eyed Sam, Big Jim, and Pete were leaning against some nearby spruces. Pete, in his dark green flannel, pulled a cigarette from his lips and blew smoke in our direction. The others just stared.

They were the wounded war heroes from World War II. One-Eyed Sam lost his eye over in Guam, fighting the Japanese. Big Jim came back with a crooked leg from the march in the Philippines. I couldn't remember what happened to Pete, but he had served on the *USS South Dakota* battleship.

"Are we in trouble?" Leroy asked the men. "It was Skipper's idea." Skipper slugged him in the shoulder.

We waited. Their silence scared us.

"Nope," Pete said, putting the cigarette back to his lips.

"You did good," One-Eyed Sam said, and signaled *let's go* to the others. As they moved back into the trees, Big Jim remained behind.

"You fought a good fight," said Big Jim. "Just remember to take the fort with you before Jenkins finds it."

Then they disappeared below the hill.

Later that evening, I stood in front of our old woodstove and told Daddy, Mama, and Chich about the warriors' visit.

Mama's concern was elsewhere. "You know Mr. Jenkins could have you all arrested," she said. "How many times have I told you not to go there?"

Daddy sipped his coffee. "Oh, Cate, I used to play there with Harlin. He never called the law. Threatened us, but never called."

"You never know. He might someday."

While Mama and Daddy discussed the pros and cons of playing in the field, I sat down on the floor next to Peewee. She added a deep blue puzzle piece to an ocean scene of palm trees and sand. Chich's sewing machine rumbled rhythmically in the corner.

"I wonder why the warriors were watching us," Peewee asked. "They never said anything until we noticed them."

Chich pulled out her scissors and began cutting stray threads from a pair of pants she was hemming for Daddy.

When I was your age and going to the old elementary school, some older warriors watched me and my cousins making doll-sized villages near the school fence one day. We stole bits of fabric, thread, and some buttons from the teacher's sewing box. Then we built miniature plankhouses out of tiny cedar sticks and made horses out of bunchgrass. We brought our cattail dolls from home. When it was all set, we pretended the tiny village was alive. The women dried river eels on racks. The men rode horses and played a stick game.

One recess we came out and noticed the men stooping down behind the fence, staring at our village. They never said a word, but they were really having a look at it. The teacher started to walk over and shoo them away. She thought they would scare us. But my cousins and I begged her not to. We wanted them to look.

"Why did you stop the teacher from chasing them away?" I asked.

Chich smiled. "Because we knew why they were looking at our village."

"You did?" said Peewee.

"Yes, because it reminded them of our ancestors' stories and how life used to be before the white men came and forced us to move."

◎ ◎ ◎

Back on the porch on 58th Place, sitting and remembering all this, I felt farther away from Grand Ronde than ever. I never lived on our rez before the white settlers. I never knew what it was like to have horses or wear beaded dresses. And I didn't live on the rez now. I lived in a new neighborhood that didn't understand warriors or the history of my people. They didn't understand why my ancestors needed to win against the cowboys. This neighborhood only knew what was told to them in movies and television and history books.

That Indians always lose.

13

BUDLONG BLUES

By Labor Day, everyone was ready for school to start. The parents. The kids. And everyone else living on 58th Place. Sunshine covered the sidewalks as our neighborhood gang of six— Keith, Addie, Anthony, Philip, Peewee, and me—headed toward Budlong Elementary School. It was just after the holiday weekend. The Santa Ana winds blew like the Chinook winds back home, only hotter. Instead of fall rains, 58th Place kept its sun and sported green grass, fresh trees, and colorful tropical flowers.

Anthony, Keith, and I were entering the school as fifth-graders. Anthony was in Miss Howard's class. Keith and I had Miss Davies.

Peewee and Addie were also in different classrooms as third-graders. And Philip, being a seventh-grader, left us at the entrance and headed toward John Muir Middle School, farther down the block.

"Too bad we're not in the same classroom," Addie said to Peewee. "But you'll love Miss Clark."

"I can't believe Budlong has two classrooms for each grade," Peewee said.

"Well, how many classrooms did your Indian school have?" Keith asked.

"Two," I answered.

"That's the same as Budlong."

"No. Two classrooms in the *entire* school," I replied.

Back on the rez, the Indian Agency school crowded grades one through seven into a before-the-turn-of-the-century schoolhouse. The younger kids, grades one through four, occupied one room, and grades five through seven crammed into the second. Pine trees outlined the schoolyard and the fish-loaded creek flowed behind.

The old fence had collapsed from lack of maintenance, but the school's bright yellow exterior was painted by the students themselves. The rain puddles in the fall and the robins singing outside the windows in the spring made us all want to be outdoors instead of reading and writing.

This school was *nothing* like that. Budlong Elementary stretched the length of a city block. The huge, three-story, red-brick building towered over the playground and was surrounded by a chain-link fence. There were one or two trees on the playground, but nothing we could climb. Worn-out asphalt, not grass, covered the ground with cracked yellow lines indicating where to play four square, hopscotch, and dodgeball. Rows of swings, monkey bars, and two lonely slides sat inside what looked like a giant sandbox.

Addie walked along with Peewee, proudly swinging her metal Disney lunch box. Peewee swung her paper-bag lunch, just as proud. "This school is huge," she said.

Students buzzed around, screaming and yelling, talking and running. Suddenly, a loud bell rang from the massive building. I jumped. Everyone froze. Another bell blared a minute later. Everyone scurried up to one of the yellow lines, filing up in rows by classroom, boys on one side and girls on the other.

"Come on, Regina," said Keith, rushing past me. "We need to line up before we get in trouble." I scooted into the girls' line for Miss Davies' class, across from him.

Teachers poured out of the building, each headed straight for their students. Miss Davies, wearing a pretty powder-blue dress with a poofy skirt and wide white belt, strolled toward us.

"Just follow the girl in front of you," whispered Keith.

A girl put her finger to her mouth. "Shush. No talking in line."

The day went by all right until Miss Davies assigned the line-shusher to me as my classroom buddy. I wasn't crazy about that. The line-shusher told me her name was Alice and scrunched her nose every time she looked at me, and she only talked to her friends.

I wanted to be with Keith instead. After all, he had become my friend that summer, and we were in the same class.

I stopped him on our way out to recess. "What do you want to do at recess?" I asked.

Keith nervously looked down at his sneakers. "I can't play with you, Regina," he said, grabbing his jacket from the classroom hook.

I stared at him in shock. "Why?"

He glanced at some boys waiting for him at the door. They giggled and pointed at us. "I just can't. Okay?" Then he left.

I stood there, not knowing what to do.

"Girls don't play with boys, silly," said Alice, who had annoyingly appeared at my side. "And you can't play with me either. I'm already late for four square."

She scampered out the door, snickering with her friends. Some classroom buddy she was.

"Run along, Regina," Miss Davies said, urging me outside.

But I didn't want to go outside. Apparently, boys and girls didn't play with one another at school here. Break the rule and get teased. It was obvious Keith didn't want that.

I finally went and looked for Peewee. She always made friends easier than I did. I didn't know if it was being older than my classmates because of my early birthday or because, like Mama said, I thought about things a lot. Sure enough, I found Peewee laughing and jumping rope with a few girls from her class.

I ended up strolling around the perimeter of the playground. I watched boys bounce a ball against a large wall and girls hopping front and back on hopscotch squares. I stood nearby, wondering if they'd invite me to join in, but they didn't.

Life at Budlong Elementary was not like 58th Place, and not at all like life back home. No trees, no creek, no robins, no playing with anyone you wanted to and lots of other rules I didn't understand. I wasn't sure I'd ever figure out how to live here.

14
MISS ELSIE'S HOUSE

After school, Mama and Miss Elsie waited by the school gate. When I asked Keith why kids called his mama Miss Elsie and not Mrs. Bates, he said it was just something they did back in Arkansas.

As we all turned onto 58th Place, we waved good-bye to the Hernández brothers and then continued to Miss Elsie's and Mr. Bates's house.

Dozens of rose bushes, all perfectly arranged, filled the front lawn. Yellow ones. Red ones. Big bright pink ones. Circling the concrete porch were pansies and multi-colored snapdragons.

"Do you have a vegetable garden too?" I asked Miss Elsie.

"No, I don't grow vegetables. Just flowers," she said, smiling proudly. She turned to Mama. "Cate, would you and the girls like to come inside, and we can have a cup of coffee?"

Would I ever? I thought. I screamed inside with happiness when Mama said yes.

I hadn't been inside anyone's house since we moved to 58th Place. Like Addie at our house that first day we met, my curiosity was piqued to see how the Bates family lived. Even though their house didn't look a lot bigger than ours, I could tell it was nicer just from the outside.

As soon as we walked inside, I saw how right I was.

Us kids settled in the family room, eating ham-and-cheese sandwiches off a pretty plate on top of a glass coffee table. Miss Elsie pulled the lacy curtains back, which let sunlight sparkle through the glass vases full of cut roses. Professional family pictures lined the walls, along with paintings of outdoor scenery. I could tell Mr. Bates had a good job at the post office. I hoped Daddy would get one too after he finished school.

Miss Elsie also had a special room no one could enter. In there, white plush couches with matching chairs, all covered in plastic, sat next to matching brown end tables holding shiny brass lamps with plastic-covered white lampshades. Very fancy.

"Has anyone ever sat in that room?" I asked.

"Yeah," Keith said. "At Christmas and New Year's."

Miss Elsie turned on a radio. Music filled the house while she and Mama drank coffee from matching cups and talked in the kitchen.

"Oh, how the Platters can sing," I heard Miss Elsie say.

"They do sound nice," Mama said.

"Mama, can we go out back?" Kevin shouted to the kitchen.

"Yes. Just remember to wipe your feet if you have to come back in for any reason."

There definitely wasn't room for a garden behind the house. A brightly colored swing set with two swings, a teeter-totter, a slide, and a hanging bar filled the space. Peewee and I loved playing on that swing set. We definitely weren't ready to go back to our side of the street when Mama stuck her head out to say we needed to head home. When we left, Miss Elsie was cooking pork chops for dinner. My mouth watered.

But their house was not our house.

15
PORK CHOPS FOR DINNER

After leaving Miss Elsie's house, I couldn't look at ours the same way. The patchy grass and empty flowerbed somehow looked worse than it had earlier that morning.

"Mama, can we have flowers too?" I asked.

"No money for that right now, Regina," Mama said. "Maybe in the spring."

On our concrete porch, a chipped metal rocker sat alone. Mama had found it near a trash can and made Daddy bring it home. She wanted to sit outside with her coffee and cigarette in the morning.

The inside of our house didn't have the beauty of Miss Elsie's either. The couch Addie had once complained about now had white doilies that Chich had crocheted to hide the frayed armrests. Mama had added unmatched chairs and side tables from the Salvation Army store. Chich had made curtains from a big bolt of muslin fabric that Mama had found on sale in another store. The house looked better than when we moved in, but that wasn't saying much.

That night, fried baloney and potatoes were served at dinner, a staple at mealtime.

"Why don't we have knickknacks like Miss Elsie's house?" I asked, pushing my food around. "And how come we don't ever have pork chops for dinner?"

"Because pork chops cost money, Regina. Be thankful we're eating this." Mama pressed her lips together. Chich sipped her coffee.

Daddy changed the subject. "Hey, did I tell you that I got top grades in my class?"

Daddy had started his trade schooling a month before Peewee and I entered Budlong. He took the No. 5 bus from Western Avenue to Westchester, some two towns away. He brought home big red books and tons of papers, and Mama had saved enough money to buy him some special pencils and drafting tools.

"If I keep doing this well, I'll end up being the top in my class at graduation."

"Really?" I said.

"That's good, tənəs-man," said Chich.

"Does that mean when you graduate, we will be able to buy pork chops for dinner?" Peewee asked, enjoying her potatoes with catsup.

"We can buy a whole pig if we want to," Daddy said. Peewee and I laughed.

"What would we do with a pig?" Mama murmured. "Where on Earth would we put it?"

"Cate, it's a joke."

"Well, I'm not laughing," she said as she pushed herself away from the table. She stacked the plates in the sink and headed to their bedroom. Daddy followed.

"Mama's upset," Peewee said. "Did I say something wrong?"

Chich stroked her cheek.

"No, kʰwiʔim. Your mama is just tired, that's

all. Why don't you and your sister go into the living room? Draw some pretty pictures so we can put them up on the wall."

"I'll work on a puzzle. Then I can glue the pieces together and hang it up," Peewee said.

Chich nodded. "Mama would like that."

Suddenly Chich held her chest. From her apron pocket, she pulled out the small medicine bottle with her heart pills. She placed a tiny white one under her tongue and closed her eyes.

"Are you all right?" I asked. "Want me to get Daddy?"

Chich shook her head and slowly got up to go to our bedroom. She had been taking those pills more often than usual since we moved to Los Angeles.

Peewee worked on her puzzle while I outlined a picture of our old farmhouse in black crayon. Voices seeped out from Mama's and Daddy's bedroom—they was muffled, but I could hear "ugly house" and "want to go home."

Back on the rez, our farmhouse wasn't glamorous either. But it was comfy. Chich's colorful quilts draped over the homemade furniture Chup had built. He'd carved eagles and bears into the legs of tables. I loved to watch him work, but I liked sewing with Chich the best.

Our walls there were covered with pictures I made at school and old black and white photos of family. One photograph showed Chup in a Grand Ronde band uniform, holding a big horn with other Indians. A hunting rifle with a detailed carving on the stock had also hung on the wall with honor.

The house had almost always smelled of baking bread, huckleberry or blackberry pies, and stews. The old wood stove churned up enough heat to keep everyone warm. I knew we were poor in Grand Ronde, but I hadn't felt poor.

I'd felt proud.

But I didn't feel that way on 58th Place.

16

HALLOWEEN CARNIVAL

By October, walking to school was a breeze. Our group stopped at every street corner and waited for the crossing guard's permission to go across busy Normandie Boulevard. Then we'd head all the way down to Budlong Avenue to arrive at school. We could do it blindfolded.

All everyone talked about at school was Halloween and the upcoming carnival. I couldn't say I understood all the excitement, because our school back home had never had one. Then again, we didn't celebrate Halloween. Now the big day had arrived, and I'd soon find out for myself.

"What's that lady doing?" I asked Keith as we all walked onto the school playground.

A woman was bent down, painting squares within an oval on the pavement near the cafeteria. Grown-ups, parents or otherwise, didn't usually come to school. And as far as I knew, they certainly weren't allowed to paint on the playground. This looked strange.

"She's part of the PTA. Gettin' ready for the cakewalk," Keith said.

"What's a cakewalk?"

"One of the carnival games. It's a big deal. You walk around the oval while music plays. When it stops, you have to stand on a square. Then they draw a number. If you're standing on it, you win a cake."

"As in birthday cakes?" Peewee asked, the Halloween birthday girl.

"As in all kinds of cakes," Addie said.

That explained why Mrs. Shapiro, the PTA chair, had asked Mama and Chich if they could each bake a cake.

Hammering echoed throughout the playground. Other parents built plywood booths near the school cafeteria.

"Did you have a Halloween carnival at your old school?" asked Addie.

"Nope," Peewee said. "But I'm excited for this one!"

"We never celebrated Halloween on our reservation," I said.

More parents arrived to decorate already-constructed booths with black-and-orange crepe paper and signs.

Even though I still couldn't figure out the real source of the excitement, I had noticed all any of the kids seemed to care about was their Halloween costumes and finding out what everyone else was going to wear.

"I'm going to dress up as the Lone Ranger," Keith said. "Why don't you come as Tonto?"

Keith had told me *The Lone Ranger* was one of his favorite television shows. I wasn't familiar with the Lone Ranger or Tonto, seeing as we didn't own a television. But I said okay. Tonto was supposed to be an Indian on the show. I was an Indian. Easiest costume ever.

Wrong.

"I told you I wanted to be Tonto—an Indian," I said later that afternoon as Chich wound my long braids into a bun.

"No," she replied. Mama had asked Chich to create costumes for Peewee and me to wear for the carnival. She'd made us each red yarn wigs to wear on our heads with white aprons to wear over dresses we already had, so we'd look like these Raggedy Ann dolls we'd seen at the store.

"But Keith wants me to be Tonto. He's dressing up as the Lone Ranger. I can't be Tonto if I go as a doll."

"Is that so? Still no."

"Why not?" I huffed.

"Because you're already an Indian," she said. "You don't need to parade as one."

Ouch. I remembered Chich's story about her grandmother and the white people staring at her like a circus act. But this was different. I would be dressing up as a TV character, not a real Indian.

But it wasn't different to Chich.

"Just like those white people who watched my grandmother dance and knew nothing about her culture or traditional dress, people around here don't know anything about Umpquas or any other tribes. They only see white actors dressed up to play 'Indians' in movies or TV shows. None of that is real." She paused and looked at me. "I want you to enjoy the carnival with your friends, but I want you to respect your family and culture too." Then she nodded for Peewee and me to get ready.

We put on our dresses and the aprons Chich had made. Then she put the yarn wigs on our heads. Mama followed her with makeup, drawing a few dark brown lines under our eyes to make large eyelashes. Next, she put some red rouge on our cheeks. Finally, she painted our lips with her "Blue Flame" red lipstick.

Reluctantly, I trailed behind as my family entered the playground that afternoon. The gray skies and winds that had hung around that morning gave way to sun and a light breeze. Elvis Presley's "All Shook Up" blasted from tall black speakers. Tons of bright crepe paper waved from colorful booths full of activities.

My classmate Richard, dressed as Superman, threw darts at balloons attached to a plywood booth. Each balloon held a strip of paper that listed what prize you won. He received a little sawdust-filled stuffed elephant.

Keith appeared in front of me in his white cowboy hat, black mask, and a black scarf around his neck. He folded his arms. "You told me you were coming as Tonto."

"I *wanted* to, but Chich said no."

"Raggedy Ann?"

"Mama made me." I sighed.

Keith turned and headed over to the fishbowl booth. I saw him try to toss ping-pong balls into glass bowls to win a goldfish. But my nose led me to the table filled with sacks of buttery popcorn, where I picked up one each for Peewee and me.

Peewee then followed Mama and Daddy to the auction booth. Mama picked up a semi-new table lamp for fifty cents. Daddy found a brand-new lock wrench for the bargain price of two dollars.

The four of us gathered together when Chich took her chance at the cakewalk. Chich gave her ticket to one of the PTA moms and stepped onto a square. Kids and parents stood on the remaining squares. Then the music started, and everyone walked around the oval. When the music stopped, Chich ended up on the square marked "three." The woman dipped her hand inside a box and pulled out . . . number three!

Peewee and I cheered. Mama clapped. And Chich received her prize. Only it was the very cake that she made the day before!

Daddy laughed. "At least we know it'll taste good."

After Peewee and I played some games ourselves, our family headed home for dinner and to have Chich's prize as Peewee's birthday cake. I munched on a caramel-covered apple on a stick as we walked. Keith had given me the goldfish in a bag he'd won to say he understood about the costume. It was the best time of my life since moving to 58th Place.

Then came Halloween night.

17
TRICK OR TREAT

"I still don't like the girls trick-or-treating," Mama said to Daddy over dinner. "Why on Earth would people start a custom of teaching their children to knock on people's doors and beg?"

We never trick-or-treated on the rez. Nobody even mentioned it. In any case, Mama wasn't convinced to let us go with our neighbor friends that night.

So I said something completely against my beliefs. "But Daddy, you said moving here makes us Americans now. And American kids trick-or-treat."

There. I did it. I bargained my Indianness for free candy.

"That's true. Go enjoy." Daddy winked at us as he headed off to catch the bus for night class.

Shortly after that, Miss Elsie, dressed in tan plaid slacks and a matching brown knitted sweater, came to the door with Keith and Addie. She told Mama she would walk all us kids around our block since Mr. Bates was home sick.

Addie looked pretty in her princess costume. Anthony was dressed up as a pirate, complete with eye patch and plastic sword. And Philip was transformed into Count Dracula, startling poor Peewee when we stopped by the Hernández house to get them before we set out. Keith still had on his same Lone Ranger costume, and Peewee and I were still dressed as Raggedy Ann dolls.

With a half-moon overhead, a warm breeze at our backs and pillowcases in hand, our group headed across 58th Place in search of candy. The overhead street lamps lit the sidewalk and road. Porch lights welcomed us to houses that had sweet loot.

Freshly made chocolate chip cookies and gifts of big chocolate bars fell into our bags. Large popcorn balls in waxed paper plopped inside our pillowcases. What a haul!

After leaving the last house on the block, I suggested we go over to the next block to get more candy. Everyone agreed and begged Miss Elsie to visit a few more houses.

"All right, but just one more block and then I take you all home."

We started down the next street, checking one another's pillowcases and sharing what we had. So far, Halloween was the best holiday yet.

From out of nowhere, eggs flew above our heads. At first, I stood dumbfounded, not understanding what was happening. Philip and Anthony ducked behind a palm tree. I saw Miss Elsie shield Addie with her body. So I jumped in front of Peewee, spreading my arms out like an idiot. Eggs splattered everywhere. One missed me—barely. Two eggs busted open on the bottom of Miss Elsie's slacks while yolk dripped off Keith's cowboy hat.

No one had noticed the blue station wagon full of four white teenage boys.

"Having fun now?!" Then the boys yelled a word I'd never heard. "You niggers!" Keith's eyes opened wide in fear. They laughed and shouted even more words I'd never heard. Words I knew meant they hated us. Then the car roared to life and sped away, tires squealing. Red taillights faded down the street.

Silence hovered in the air.

I trembled. My eyes filled.

Addie looked at Miss Elsie and bawled. Keith stood stunned. The Hernández brothers came out slowly from behind the palm trees.

Then Peewee choked out between sobs, "I w-w-want my m-m-mama!"

"We're all going home, baby," Miss Elsie whispered as she knelt to wipe the dripping egg from her slacks onto the grass. She rose up and touched Peewee's cheek with her shaky hand. "Let's all get moving quick, okay?" With a clenched jaw, she scanned the street and shepherded us back toward our block on 58th Place. I held Peewee's hand tight.

We moved fast. When we arrived at Anthony's

and Philip's house, Miss Elsie informed Mrs. Hernández about the egging. Mrs. Hernández covered her mouth and said something in Spanish that caused the brothers' eyes to widen and look at each other. She patted Miss Elsie's shoulder and then hurried the boys inside.

Then we got to our house. Mama sat smoking a cigarette in her rocker on the porch. I glanced down fast. I didn't want her to know I was scared. But Peewee rushed up and sobbed right into her lap.

"I'm so sorry, Cate. Something awful happened," Miss Elsie began and told her all about how the white boys in the station wagon threw eggs and said awful words.

First, Mama asked Miss Elsie if she was all right. Miss Elsie responded that she was ready to get herself, Keith, and Addie home. Next, Mama thanked her for taking us trick-or-treating and bringing us home.

But as soon as she closed the door and knew Miss Elsie was across the street, the screaming began. Most in Portuguese and some in English.

Mama waved her hands with her cigarette circling like a glowing sparkler.

Then Daddy walked in the door from class.

Mama gave him an earful.

"It's all right, Cate," Daddy said, putting down his things. "You girls didn't get hurt, did you?"

We stayed quiet, but shook our heads no.

"Why don't you two show me what you got?" Chich said, touching our cheeks to calm our fears.

She went into our room and returned with some fabric for us to sort out all the goodies inside our pillowcases on the floor.

We did as we were told, showing Chich each kind of treat we had. Chocolate was put in one stack, bubble gum in another, baked treats, and so on. We kept our heads down, though, not daring to look up at Mama. She relayed to Daddy everything Miss Elsie shared about the incident. I wondered about that word those boys kept saying.

"Maybe we should think about moving to another area," Daddy said. "You know, living here makes us guilty by association."

"Guilty of what?" Mama snapped.

Daddy stayed quiet and glanced at us girls as he swiped a chocolate bar from my pile. I wanted to protest but thought better of it.

"Mama," I asked, "what's a nigger?"

She spun around fast. "Regina Petit! I better never hear that word from your lips again! Do you hear me?"

Cowering, I nodded. Tears filled my eyes again.

"It's a very bad word! A filthy name!"

"I promise," I whispered, just before Mama and Daddy headed into their bedroom.

I still didn't know what it meant. What I did know was that I had caused this. If I hadn't asked if we could go trick-or-treating for another block in the first place, nobody would have been egged, I would never have heard that word, and Mama and Daddy wouldn't be fighting in the bedroom now about moving.

"It's time for bed, girls," Chich said, helping us move our stash of goodies into the kitchen. She then removed our yarn wigs and took a warm wet cloth to our faces to remove our makeup.

Then she sent us off to have a bath. After we had washed away any physical reminders of the day, Chich took time with each of us, drying and combing our hair.

I felt better, but sleep did not come easy. My mind kept seeing egg yolk hanging off Keith's hat along with Addie and Peewee crying their eyes out. I didn't understand everything that happened. But I knew two things. I would apologize to Keith and his family the next day. And this was the first and last time we'd ever celebrate Halloween.

18

AN INDIAN LIKE TONTO

November brought its own mix of good and bad to our lives on 58th Place.

First, Daddy graduated from his technical school and got two diplomas in the mail. He received the highest marks in his class, just like he'd said he would, making him the top pick for companies hiring.

Tele-Autograph, a very large electronics firm, recruited him after graduation. The company designed mechanical writing equipment that could send people's signatures from one office to another. According to Daddy, it was revolutionary stuff.

"I'll be making good money, more than we

ever had before." Daddy beamed. Mama had saved enough money from the government's allotment to buy him two pairs of black trousers, three white long-sleeved button-down shirts, and one thin black tie at the J.C. Penney's down on Rosecrans Avenue.

That must be why we had eaten so much fried baloney.

On his first day at work, Daddy stepped out in his new outfit—way spiffier than his logging clothes back home.

"You look very handsome," Mama said, handing him a cup of black coffee, which he accepted. Then he snuck a kiss.

"Proud of you, tənəs-man," Chich said.

I wanted to say something too. "You look just like an Indian agent."

Daddy laughed. "Well, I hope I do a better job at helping folks than they ever did." He hugged Peewee and me before we headed out to meet everyone and walk to school. Daddy still caught the No. 5 bus to Westchester to get to his new job.

As our group walked home from school that afternoon, Keith walked fast, saying he didn't want to miss *The Lone Ranger*. "Let me ask my mom if you can come over and watch it."

"That'd be great. I've never seen it."

"What? How?"

"We don't have a television," I whispered, so the other kids wouldn't hear me. "You've been to my house, remember?"

"But you didn't even have one back home?"

"No, never."

There. I confessed. We hardly ever had anything anyone here did. Back on the rez, there was no need for a TV. We spent time outside, and during bad weather, we drew, read, or played games inside.

When we got to our street, Keith ran inside to ask Miss Elsie. She said both Peewee and I were invited to watch an episode and stay for dinner. Mama agreed to let us go.

Dinner consisted of pot roast, mashed potatoes, and something called greens. It smelled sort of like the cooked spinach they served at school, but Keith assured me it wasn't. They said a prayer before the meal, but it wasn't the Catholic one we said over meals. And it was longer than what I was used to, thanking the Lord for about everything that happened that day.

After dinner, Miss Elsie served dessert in the living room. Us kids sat on the floor behind the coffee table. Mr. Bates walked over to the television set, turned the knob on, and adjusted the antenna on top until the black-and-white picture cleared up.

Trumpets blared, and fast-paced music played from the TV, which was showing a white cowboy in a black mask riding a pure white horse. Then a voice declared:

> *With his faithful Indian companion Tonto, the daring and resourceful masked rider of the plains led the fight for law and order in the early western United States . . .*

Next a *real* Indian appeared, not some white actor with fake black braids and painted skin like Daddy said played most Indian parts in

Hollywood. Tonto wore a fringed shirt and pants, which swayed with each footstep. Leather moccasins covered his feet. He had a thin leather strap tied around his forehead. And he owned a horse, Scout, a gorgeous paint pony. The actor's name, Jay Silverheels, appeared on the screen. Mr. Bates said he read in an interview with Jay Silverheels that he came from the Mohawk tribe.

I hadn't heard of that one, but I was in love!

In this episode, the Lone Ranger and Tonto entered an Indian reservation where everyone owned horses. *Even* the young Indian boys!

Then I noticed the white actors spoke perfect English. However, the Indians, including Tonto, spoke broken English. No way had I ever heard any Indian talk like that. It sounded weird. But Tonto was still my hero!

"I can see why you like this show so much," I told Keith after it ended.

Peewee and I thanked Miss Elsie and Mr. Bates before returning our plates and cups to the kitchen. We raced across the street and flew through the front door.

Daddy and Mama sat on the couch. Daddy lowered the newspaper as Mama looked up from a murder mystery she had checked out at the John Muir Library nearby.

"Daddy! Daddy! I know what I want to be when I grow up!"

He tilted his head to the side. "Okay. I'll bite. What do you want to be when you grow up?" Daddy asked, paying full attention.

I grinned. "I want to be an Indian when I grow up!"

Daddy and Mama stared at me, then at each other. Mama reached over to tap the ashes from her cigarette into the ashtray. "What?" she asked again.

"I want to be an Indian."

Daddy slapped his knee and howled with laughter. Mama worked hard not to smile and took a sip of coffee.

"Girl, you're already an Indian," Daddy said, still laughing and wiping his eyes.

I slumped to the floor. "Not that kind of Indian," I moaned. "An Indian like Tonto. He wears Indian clothing with moccasins. He even has a beautiful paint pony. In fact, all the Indians on TV have horses."

Daddy smiled, motioning me to him. "If we were that kind of Indian, where would we put all our horses? In our tiny backyard?"

I folded my arms.

"Horses need a lot of land, sweetie. Maybe when you're older, you can buy a horse. Though for the life of me, I don't know where you would put it in Los Angeles."

"When I'm older, I plan to go back home," I muttered. "Then I'll have all the land I need."

"We'll see."

"Can we buy a TV, Daddy?" Peewee asked.

"Yeah, and you could watch *The Lone Ranger* to see what I'm talking about!" I added.

"Televisions cost a lot of money," Mama said. "Maybe one day."

◎ ◎ ◎

That "one day" came sooner than I thought. A couple of weeks before Thanksgiving, Daddy carried home a television set.

"I bought it from this guy for fifteen dollars," he said. He carefully placed it in the corner of the living room and maneuvered the set like he was going to turn it on. "I plan on fixing it."

"It doesn't work? That's a lot of money for something that doesn't work," said Mama.

"Trust me, I'll get it to work."

Mama, Chich, Peewee, and I watched him as he traveled from the living room into the tiny laundry room and brought back his prized toolbox that Tele-Autograph had given him. For the rest of that evening, Daddy scattered the television's guts all over the wooden floor. He carefully dusted off each tube and studied each circuit board.

"You *are* going to clean everything up when you're done, aren't you?" Mama asked as Daddy tested another tube.

"Don't worry, Cate," he said.

Mama checked each morning to make sure Daddy hadn't left any television parts on the floor. It seemed he buried his head deep inside the body of the set, working on it any minute he had free.

I didn't know if Daddy could make that TV work. But I knew I wanted to watch Jay Silverheels play Tonto if he did!

19
THE JACKET

While Daddy tinkered with the television, Chich kept me busy helping her with a sewing project.

Mrs. Hernández had rushed over one evening with a size forty-two man's jacket. "Philip's confirmation at St. John's is scheduled just before Thanksgiving. We don't have money to buy him a new jacket, but I found this beautiful black wool one at the secondhand store," she explained. "Would you be able to make this a little smaller? I know it's short notice. I understand if you can't do it."

Everyone on the street knew Chich sewed. Since we moved to 58th Place, she had made a dress for Addie, curtains for Mrs. Gartner, the elderly German woman across the street, and repaired a zipper on Miss Elsie's blue linen dress. Our living room was also looking better each month. Beautiful new curtains hung on our windows.

"I will do my best," she said, looking over the jacket. "I need to measure Philip first."

Mrs. Hernández returned with Philip, and Chich took his measurements. After they left, she went into the kitchen to get a few paper grocery bags to make a pattern.

It had been a while since I offered to help Chich with a sewing project, and I missed it. "Can I help with the jacket, Chich?"

She smiled. "Of course, kʰwiʔim." She put me to work carefully ripping out the seams that held the jacket together while she drew a boy's jacket pattern on paper grocery bags. Pieces of brown paper lay everywhere.

"Bring those old jacket pieces," she said, "and let's start pinning the pattern on them."

I watched her first. She placed the pattern

on the fabric, pinning it down. I then took one of the sleeves and placed the pattern and the pins just as Chich had. Once all the pattern pieces were pinned, we took turns using the scissors to carefully cut the excess material away from the pattern.

"Where did you learn to sew?" I asked.

My mother taught me. She had learned to sew when she and the other kids from the reservation were forced to go to boarding school. Said it was the only thing she enjoyed there. The schoolteachers wouldn't allow the children to speak Umpqua or sing our songs. She realized that no one bothered her when she spent hours at the sewing machine, so she would hum the melodies to our songs and sing them in her head. She told herself our stories in Umpqua over and over again, so she wouldn't forget. It helped her feel connected to home because she rarely got to visit her family.

Next, Chich stitched together the newly trimmed black wool fabric pieces with her Singer sewing machine. Then it was time to make the lining.

She showed me how to take the same pattern pieces and make them smaller. We placed them on the blue-striped satin fabric and pinned and cut those as well.

This time she had me take a few turns sitting down at the sewing machine to sew some pieces. Together we sewed up the blue-striped lining.

I loved sitting next to Chich each night, working away on Philip's jacket. Like her mother, she'd be humming or singing songs in our language from back home.

The night before we were to give the jacket to Mrs. Hernández, Chich guided me as I hand-stitched the lining inside it. "Make sure to hide your stitches so they don't show," she said, taking time to review my work when I got lost in my thoughts. "Good, very good."

When Mrs. Hernández came back with Philip, Chich brought out the jacket.

Mrs. Hernández teared up, her hands covering her mouth. "¡Magnífico!" she whispered, motioning for Philip to put it on. He reluctantly obeyed, pushing his arms into the sleeves of the jacket over his white T-shirt. Not only did it fit, but it looked like it had always been a boy's jacket. "How much?"

"Nothing," Chich said, smiling at our creation and back at me. "It's a gift."

"¡Ay, qué generosa!" Mrs. Hernández clutched her heart. "If you ever need anything, anything at all, please ask. Muchas gracias."

20

PILGRIMS & INDIANS

Sometimes Budlong Elementary felt like the boarding school that Chich's mother had gone to long ago. No one seemed to respect our language, culture or stories. We celebrated Thanksgiving at Budlong, another holiday no one back home in Grand Ronde observed. The teachers at school prepared a play where classes acted out various parts of the "First Thanksgiving" celebration. They sorted students according to who would be best as Pilgrims and Indians. Guess which part I got to play?

"I wouldn't laugh if I were you," Keith said, annoyed at my chuckling over his tall, black-buckled hat and oversized white collar.

He grabbed my fake buckskin vest, made from a brown grocery sack, and accidently pulled off one of the paper fringes. "I hate my lines in this play."

"Too bad you can't wear your real Indian costume," Richard said as he passed by, sporting a multicolor construction-paper headdress and a brown-paper-bag vest nearly identical to mine. Mine had Keith's bright crayon drawing of "Indian" symbols he learned through Boy Scouts, which looked nothing like those I knew from home.

I sighed. "We don't wear costumes, Richard. It's awful we have to wear these silly paper bags at all."

"Why, you look just like a real Indian," said one of the mothers helping us get ready. She fingered my braids and then painted red lines on both my cheeks with her lipstick. I stared down at the classroom floor.

"That's because she is," said Alice, smirking in the Pilgrim costume her mother made. She twirled around in a long black dress with a white apron and bonnet.

Mama, Chich, and Miss Elsie came to our afternoon performance in Budlong's auditorium. Each grade had a five-minute segment to present as part of the First Thanksgiving story. Here at Budlong, the way each grade had their classes perform, you would think that the Indians were starving before the white men arrived and that the Pilgrims came to *their* rescue.

For the fourth grade, Addie's class sang a song about how the Indians danced for the Pilgrims at the celebration, whooping and leaping around in a circle. I'd never seen or heard about any Indian dancing like the song described. Peewee's class selected her to share the drawing she made demonstrating how the Indians lived *before* the Pilgrims' ship landed. She drew mothers cooking, fathers bringing in fish, and kids playing. At least that seemed true.

Our class followed with Richard, our "chief," leading twelve of us "Indians" onstage. He strutted around, nodding to each of us. Then Miss Davies gave us the signal to sit on the floor, legs crossed.

The Pilgrims, headed by Keith and Alice,

came onstage. "Chief" Richard got up to meet them.

"Thank you for inviting us to join you," said Keith.

"Welcome to this land," Richard replied.

Keith nervously adjusted his big collar and hat. The hat was slipping down on his ears. I giggled. He screwed up his nose at me before looking back at Richard. "Your people and my people will share bread on this day," he said. "You will teach us how to plant corn and pumpkins."

"And we who are civilized will teach you our ways," added Alice, handing over a Bible, "so you will become civilized too."

Then the Pilgrims placed a long table on the stage. Keith stood at the head of it, semi-mumbling, "Thank you, God, for allowing us to teach these savages our ways. Amen."

Us "Indians" then had to get up and do a "welcome dance" that, again, didn't look like anything I had heard of or seen back home.

I glanced up and saw Chich's back stiffen as she watched us.

As we all walked home, Chich put one of those little white pills under her tongue to settle her heart while Mama and Miss Elsie walked quietly behind us. No one wanted to talk about the play, and I was fine with that. I tried rubbing the red stripes off my cheeks, but nothing worked. Once we got inside the house, Chich smoothed Mama's cold cream on them and the lipstick came right off. But I wasn't sure I'd ever forget this day or what those stripes felt like.

21

THANKSGIVING DAY

Despite what had happened at school, Thanksgiving went way better at home.

Early Thanksgiving morning, Daddy shook our bed and flipped back our quilts. "Get up or you'll miss it!"

I rubbed my eyes as my feet touched the cool wooden floor. "We'll miss what?" I mumbled.

"Hurry!"

Peewee and I dragged our half-awake bodies into the living room. The smell of a roasting turkey filled the air.

And now here comes Popeye, flexing his muscles down Broadway in New York City!

The television, that previously dead box with spilled innards, displayed a giant balloon of this cartoon character—complete with corncob pipe and anchors tattooed on his arms, squinting one eye. So many people were needed to hold the balloon close to the ground with long ropes.

"You got the television to work!" I shouted. I'd known Daddy was smart, but I hadn't known he was that smart.

Chich poked her head in from the kitchen just in time for another balloon to pass across the screen. "It almost looks like you're right there," she said, holding some unpeeled potatoes.

Peewee and I grabbed our cornflakes and sat on the floor to watch the rest of the parade. We hollered toward the kitchen every time a big float or another balloon passed in front of the camera. A group of dancers called the Rockettes performed for the first time at the parade. Wow, could they kick high!

Our eyes never left the screen. The announcer said this was the Macy's Thanksgiving Day Parade. We watched until the parade ended when a bearded white man named Santa Claus and his reindeer stopped in front of Macy's Department Store.

"Can we watch something else?" I asked.

"Ask your father," Mama said. "I haven't the foggiest idea of how to work that thing."

Daddy went over and turned the channel knob around. He stopped on a station with cartoons, which looked like moving comic-book images to me. I sat spellbound and didn't move until noon, when Mama demanded we come and have dinner.

"John, you give grace," Mama said, finally sitting down at the table.

"All righty," Daddy said, putting down his fork. "We give thanks for good food. Good meat. Good God. Let's eat."

"John!"

"Regina, would you please lead us in prayer?" Mama said in a huff.

"Bless us, oh Lord, and these thy gifts, which we are about to receive from thy bounty, through

 126

Christ our Lord. Amen." I looked at everyone around the table. "Chich, are you okay?"

"Just a little tired. I'll lay down for a bit after we eat." She seemed tired more often now.

For the first time since we left Grand Ronde, food covered almost the entire table. Turkey, mashed potatoes, gravy, stuffing, corn, peas, and red Jell-O with whipped cream, my favorite dessert. Since we didn't celebrate Thanksgiving back home, Miss Elsie shared her stuffing recipe with Mama, so she'd know how to make it. It was delicious.

And that's when I knew we weren't poor anymore. No one who ate like this and owned a television could be poor.

22

LIVING THE DREAM

If getting a TV and having a full table of food wasn't enough to convince me we weren't poor anymore, then Christmas that year sure did.

"A car, John, really?" Mama said, loud enough for the entire neighborhood to hear.

Yes, just before Christmas, Daddy bought a car. It was a brown 1950 Lincoln Club coupe, complete with working headlights, real tan leather seats, and no rust spots.

"Cate," Daddy said as Mama stood on the porch with her hands on her hips, "I need a car to get to work. And we need a car to go shopping."

"I don't mind taking the bus with Miss Elsie. She's always good company."

"Well, I mind."

Peewee and I couldn't wait to climb inside. We opened the back door and sat, winding down the windows and bouncing on the seats.

"Okay, John, just how much is this going to cost us?" Mama asked.

Daddy just grinned. "Don't worry. Trust me. We can afford it."

Chich strolled around the sedan. "What's wrong with buying a used truck?" she asked.

"Look around you, Ma. People here don't drive trucks."

I leaned out the car window and searched the neighborhood. Daddy was right. Every vehicle on the street was either a Chevy, Ford, or Dodge car. Not a truck in sight.

In Grand Ronde, trucks ruled. Not only could they handle the muddy roads during the rainy season, but they could hold a whole cord of wood for winter. And two broken-down trucks could be combined into one running truck.

But this was Christmas season. Daddy got his car. Mama got to go shopping for more than two days' worth of groceries. Chich got to explore a fabric store farther away. And Peewee and I got to see Santa over at Sears.

Then, on Christmas morning, Peewee and I got more presents than we ever had before. Daddy received a few more tools and two short-sleeved white shirts. Daddy bought Mama some Jean Naté perfume, a new dress, and gold clip-on earrings. Chich got more yarn, quilting squares, needles, and a jacket-and-skirt set.

Peewee and I usually got dresses from Chich, and we did again, but this year they were made from colorful calico cloth. Daddy and Mama gave Raggedy Ann and Andy dolls with doll beds to Peewee. I got charcoal and colored pencils with some sketch pads. We both got a deck of cards to share.

"Hey, Daddy," Peewee said, holding up the cards, "now you can teach us poker."

Mama just shook her head. "Don't you dare," she warned. Daddy winked at us when she wasn't looking.

I remembered when we first arrived at 58th

Place. Daddy jokingly said moving to LA made us Americans, that soon we'd be white people, and Indian no more. Now I wondered if that all might be coming true.

23

NO SERVICE

Funny how life sometimes answers your questions sooner than you expect.

After Christmas, Daddy drove to work instead of taking the bus. Mama started waitressing Friday and Saturday nights over at Peking's Restaurant. Chich continued to sew, crochet, and cook. She also taught Peewee and me Chinuk Wawa words and symbols found in our culture like those we saw woven into baskets or carved into wood.

In other words, life was feeling a little better in Los Angeles.

"Daddy is taking us all out for dinner tonight," Mama announced in late January. She had taken the night off work.

Back in Grand Ronde, we could never afford going out for dinner, not even when Mama was working at the local diner. Sitting down for a meal at a restaurant—*wow*!

"Can I order whatever I want?" I asked, already dreaming of pork chops smothered in gravy.

"Let's see what the restaurant serves first," Chich said, brushing invisible lint from her skirt. "Did tənəs-man say why we're going out?"

"He said he would tell us at the restaurant," Mama replied, putting lipstick on and blotting her lips on a tissue.

Just thinking about going out to dinner made Peewee and me hungry. But Mama wouldn't let us have a snack in the kitchen. "You'll spoil your dinner," she said.

The winter sun had already set when Daddy finally arrived home from work. Each of us chose our new clothes from Christmas. Mama twirled around in her multicolored dress and black pumps. Chich had on her navy-blue skirt with its matching jacket. Peewee and I wore matching store-bought dresses from Sears and colorful ribbons around our long braids.

"My," Daddy said, "do I have the most beautiful girls! Good thing I'm the most handsome devil."

We piled inside the Lincoln and sang "Jailhouse Rock" along with Elvis on the car radio. Daddy drove down West Slauson Avenue. Yellow lights flickered like fireflies from billboards, lampposts, and neon signs. The busy streets sounded like rushing water with cars speeding by us. It wasn't long before Daddy was pulling in to park behind Sheri's Restaurant.

"Bert from work told me this place has the best steaks around," he said as he opened the car door for Chich and Mama.

"Oh, we have enough money for steaks?" Mama asked.

"We have enough money to buy the cow," Daddy said. "And the potato crop."

Mama took his arm and entered the restaurant through its red leather-padded doors.

Sheri's restaurant was super fancy compared

to the diner in Grand Ronde. Instead of scratched tables and chairs, red leather benches lined the walls in front of dark wooden tables topped with bright white cloths. Sparkling vases filled with flowers sat at each table. A cascade of shimmering lights drooped down from the ceiling. We walked over the richly patterned carpet that covered the floors.

"Wow," I said.

No one greeted us, so Daddy pointed to an empty booth just a few steps away. We all sat down.

"Can't wait to see what they serve," Mama said, watching one waitress carrying plates of sizzling sirloins and baked potatoes. Peewee nodded in agreement.

"You can have anything you like, baby," Daddy said. "We're celebrating." He leaned next to Mama. "Guess who's a new supervisor?"

"You got a promotion?" Mama said, giving him a peck. "So soon?"

"What can I say?" Daddy said. "I'm invaluable. And I smell nice too."

"That's because Indians don't sweat," Chich said.

Daddy chuckled. "Tonight we're rich Americans, Ma."

"Well, this place looks expensive. Hope you brought enough money," Chich said, opening her purse and taking out her wallet. I watched as she counted her bills.

"Put your money away, Ma," Daddy said. "I'm taking care of it."

While waiting for menus from the waitress, Daddy talked about his new position. "Four men now report to me. I might have to work late and on weekends, depending on the deadlines." He leaned forward. "I even have my own office."

"Will it have a desk and chair?" Peewee asked.

Daddy laughed. "Hope so!"

Mama's eyes twinkled, and Chich nodded with approval.

"Bert, one of the other managers, lives in Westchester, by the way. He says there are some really nice houses for sale," Daddy said.

"John, buying a bigger house will require a

down payment," Mama said, glancing at another waitress passing us by.

"I have the GI Bill. We can get a mortgage loan without a down payment," Daddy said as he stroked her hand.

"I don't want to move," I said without being asked. "Keith lives on 58th Place. And so do our other friends. We moved enough already."

I expected a scolding, since the rule was to never interrupt when adults were talking. Both Daddy and Mama just stared at me.

"She's right," Chich said, touching my braid. "We've moved enough already. Maybe the girls need a little more time to adjust to the city."

I smiled. Chich was on my side, though she never gave me the impression she was happy living on 58th Place or living in the city at all, except when she was helping our neighbors.

I glanced around the restaurant. Lots of people were enjoying dinner. Some old, some young and a few couples with children. I started thinking about life on the rez, only to realize I couldn't remember some details. Was I beginning to forget Grand Ronde? Maybe even being Indian?

"Daddy," I asked, "any chance we could go home for a visit, maybe?" I didn't like the idea of losing my Indianness.

"It would be nice to visit, John," Mama said, touching his hand. "For your mother and the girls?"

He looked away and sighed. "Maybe we can drive up in early August when the weather's nice."

We all smiled.

Waitresses still rushed around us, giving out menus to other customers, filling their water glasses, and taking their orders. I noticed two customers who'd arrived after us receive menus.

"John, try to get the waitress's attention," Mama whispered to Daddy.

An older blonde waitress passed our table. Daddy raised his finger to call her to the table. She stopped. "May we have our menus, please?" Daddy asked.

But the waitress just stood there. She glared at our table and huffed.

My face flushed. I rocked back and forth in my seat. I knew something was wrong, but I couldn't figure it out. Peewee looked down at her lap.

The woman's blue eyes seared into us. She leaned close in with her right hand pressed down on the table. She whispered so the other customers didn't hear. "I don't think we have anything here *you* can afford." She straightened and folded her arms. "Besides, we don't serve Mexicans here."

Mama's eyes widened. Then Daddy straightened up. "We're not Mexicans," he replied with a low, firm voice.

The white woman pursed her lips. "I don't care what you think you are. Our restaurant does not serve your kind here."

She was kicking us out. Daddy had money to pay for our meals. He rose from his seat. The waitress backed off with a frightened look. Suddenly all conversation in the restaurant stopped. I wondered what Daddy would do.

Chich motioned for us to get up.

Mama stood up next. Daddy helped her with her coat.

Anger replaced fear in me. I hated how the white waitress talked to us. I hated everyone's stares.

I grabbed my sweater and then lagged a little behind the others as we walked toward the doors. I don't know what got into me. Suddenly I whipped around. "We're not Mexicans!" I shouted at her. "We're Indians!"

Daddy reached back and snatched me by the arm, pulling me out through those red-leather doors.

24

INDIAN NO MORE

"Do you think Daddy will come back?" Peewee said to Mama.

We all wondered the same thing sitting around that rusty kitchen table. Peewee and I munched on a baloney sandwich while Mama and Chich sipped coffee.

Daddy had dropped us off in front of the house without a word. His gray eyes burned. His mouth twitched. He'd waited until we were on the sidewalk before he tore off down the street. A few neighbors peeked out from their windows.

"It's all my fault he's mad," I said, lips quivering. "I should never have said anything."

"It's not either," Chich said, stroking my

head. "The waitress was disrespectful. Your father just needs time to think."

"About what?" I asked, rubbing a tear from my cheek.

"About being Indian, I suppose," Chich said. "No matter how hard he tries, he can't ignore who he is."

"Will he ever come back?" Peewee cried. "I want my daddy."

Mama scooted her chair next to Peewee's and hugged her. "Daddy will come back. He'll be here before you know it."

"I want to go back home," I cried, wiping my nose on my sleeve. "No one treated us like this in Grand Ronde."

"Ah, but if you went just a couple miles south, on the other side of the Yamhill River, they would have. Lots of Indian men couldn't get hired to work for whites. And in Portland, it was worse," Chich said. "Some stores there even had signs saying, 'ONLY WHITES ALLOWED.' Your Daddy thinks if he works a bit harder, wears better clothes, lives in a nicer home, and buys expensive stuff, white people will respect him. But he's Indian. We're Indian. And Indians aren't white."

"I might as well tell you," Mama said to Chich, lighting up a cigarette. "John confessed that his coworkers call him 'Chief.'"

"It's always been hard for him." Chich sighed. "Ever since he was a child, he's hated being treated differently."

Mama hugged Peewee and me. "Let's all get to bed. It's late."

◎ ◎ ◎

Peewee was deep in dreams next to me, but I couldn't sleep. I worried that Daddy might get so mad he would go back and yell at the waitress and get in trouble. Or just keep driving until he was back in Grand Ronde without us.

I thought about home and how things were different there. No, we didn't have a television set. And no, Daddy didn't have a job that paid good money. But he always came home happy to see us. He told jokes, teased Mama, and played with us girls. Once he even let me paint his toe-nails with my watercolors. Before long, I drifted off to memories of running through the fields of Grand Ronde with Daddy chasing me.

In the early morning, a door slammed. I bolted up in bed. So did Chich. Peewee mumbled but remained asleep.

"What was that?" I whispered.

There was a bang against the couch and sudden cursing. Feet shuffled on the wooden floor. The overhead light turned on in the living room.

"Cate!" Daddy yelled.

"Oh no," Chich said. She flipped off her quilt. "You stay in bed."

I sat still. She wrapped her bathrobe over her nightgown and left. Then I crept out of bed and peeked out the door.

Daddy staggered about, almost tipping over Chich's sewing machine. He shook his head as he forced his eyes to focus. "Cate!"

Mama came from the kitchen, wearing her favorite red flannel nightgown. She scowled. "You're drunk. Come to bed before you wake the girls."

 144

"What? They need to wake up!" Daddy shouted. "They need to listen!" I saw him strolling over to our bedroom.

"tənəs-man, no," Chich said from just outside our bedroom door.

I stepped back, hugging myself. I didn't know what Daddy was going to do.

He passed Chich and stood in the now-open doorway, swaying back and forth. "Get your sister up."

I did what he said. Peewee wasn't too happy with me waking her up, but she quickly obeyed when she heard Daddy yelling.

"We're Americans, dammit!" His words slurred. "We're not from another country! Hell, I'm a United States veteran!"

"Please lower your voice." Mama spoke as gently as she could. "Girls, go back to bed right now. John, let's go! We can talk about this in the morning."

"I want to talk about it now!" Daddy staggered back over to Peewee and me huddled together. His breath smelled of beer.

"Girls, you might as well know, if you're Indian, you'll never get anywhere. You all listening?"

Peewee let out a small cry. I nodded, clinging closer to her.

"John," Chich said firmly, the first time I'd ever heard her use his given name, "go to bed. The girls are Indians. You can't change that."

"I can't, huh? Well, I'm not going to sit here like you and fill their heads with old stories about the past."

Daddy suddenly gripped my arm and dragged me over to Chich's sewing table. My eyes widened. I'd never seen Daddy act like this.

He found the sewing scissors and held them up. "You can't make them Indian anymore. We're terminated. We're dead. You understand that? They're American!"

Daddy pulled hair from the left side of my head. He stretched it out. His other hand held the scissors. Then he snipped. "Now she's American."

He let my hair go. It spread all over the floor. Dead.

I stared, stunned. No one moved.

Peewee shrieked. Terrified of being the next victim, she scrambled into the dark kitchen, dove under the table, and bawled, "Don't let Daddy get me. Please don't let him hurt me."

"John, what have you done?" Mama shouted in Portuguese at him with her hands flying, sobbing between words.

Tears streamed down my cheeks. I trembled uncontrollably. My heart pounded loud in my ears. I'd never felt this kind of anger before. I whipped myself around to face him. "I HATE YOU!"

I punched him in the stomach. I pushed him away from me. I screamed again, "I HATE YOU!"

I did hate him. I couldn't find all the words right then, but I hated him for cutting my hair. For not standing up to the waitress. For not standing up to the Indian agent back home. For not standing up to the government that terminated us.

"kʰəpít," Chich said, standing by the TV. "Stop," she repeated in English. "John, you've done enough. Go to bed."

After a few moments' pause, Daddy obeyed Chich without argument.

Mama scooped up Peewee from under the table and carried her to our bed, where they lay down together.

Chich hugged me and looked me in the eyes, silently telling me to be brave. Then she sat me down on one of the kitchen chairs and draped a towel around my shoulders. I could hear Daddy already snoring. Chich took the same scissors and assessed the damage. Then she snipped long strands off the other side of my head. She held them in her hand.

I worked hard not to cry, gulping in air. When she finished making both sides even, my hair barely touched my ears.

That night I became Indian no more.

25

BEAVER

Chich prepared hot oatmeal with raisins for breakfast the next morning. Usually Peewee and I slept in on Saturday mornings before enjoying our breakfasts while watching cartoons. But not this morning. I said nothing, and Peewee didn't either.

Chich was fixing coffee when suddenly her face scrunched up. She touched her side, grimacing.

Mama saw it too. "Are you all right?" she asked.

Chich's expression changed. "I'm fine," she said. She attempted a smile and turned toward me. "Do you want to greet the day?"

I shook my head. I wasn't Indian anymore. Why do Indian things?

Peewee headed over to Addie's house while I plopped down outside on the porch steps. I pulled my old blue sweater over my knees and tucked my face between them. I had no plans to see anyone. I kept pulling on my cropped hair, hoping that would make it longer.

A voice startled me. "You look like Moe from The Three Stooges."

Keith sat down beside me. I tucked my head farther down in my lap. "Shut up."

"What happened?"

I didn't answer.

"Why did you cut your hair?"

I still didn't answer. He sat down next to me.

"Was it your mom's idea?"

I lifted my head, giving Keith a look. "If you must know, my dad decided it was time to make me American." I pounded on my knees. "Like being American is so much better."

We sat there in silence for a minute. I was determined not to cry in front of him.

He put his hand on my back and changed the subject. "Philip has been working on his magic kit that he got back at Christmas. Wanna come over and see his new tricks?"

"Not really. I look like a boy now."

"You don't look like a boy. It just looks different. Come on. No one will tease you. I'll make sure of it."

Keith was ready to defend me if anyone teased me. I appreciated that. But I knew he didn't understand completely. I'd lost my hair. I'd lost my heritage. I had told Daddy I hated him. I reburied my head in my lap.

At Keith's urging, I finally agreed to go over to Philip's house. I still hated my haircut and the fact I didn't look Indian anymore. I turned up the steps to let Mama know where I was going but saw her opening the door.

"Something's wrong with Chich. She's complaining about her stomach."

Chich had never been really sick before, except for the one time her heart fluttered real bad back home. After the rez doctor gave her those little white pills to dissolve under her tongue, she hadn't gotten sick like that again.

But the look on Mama's face said everything.

"I'll go get Mrs. Hernández!" Keith shouted as he sprinted down the street.

I flew inside.

Chich moaned softly from that stained government couch, clutching her side. Her face was red. Her eyes squinted in pain.

I plopped down a little too quickly next to her. She winced. "Sorry," I said, getting up.

"No, it's okay," Chich said, patting for me to sit again.

I slowly sat next to her, not knowing what to do. Mama gave me a wet washcloth to place over Chich's forehead. "That feels good," she said. I smiled slightly.

Mrs. Hernández entered our house with her doctor's bag—and Philip, Anthony, and Keith by her side. I moved to the edge of the couch as she rummaged in her bag. Pulling out a thermometer, Mrs. Hernández took Chich's temperature and felt her wrist.

When Mrs. Hernández pressed Chich's stomach, she cried out.

"Get some ice in a bag," Mrs. Hernández ordered Mama.

Mama returned with the ice. "Regina, hold the bag here," Mrs. Hernández said. She pointed to Chich's lower abdomen.

Chich asked for some water.

"No, Mrs. Petit," Mrs. Hernández said. "It is best not to drink anything right now." She took Mama aside. "She needs to go to the hospital. I believe it's her appendix." Then she turned to Philip and said, "Señora Elsie tiene teléfono. Corra y pídale que llame la ambulancia. ¡Rápido!"

I stayed with Chich while Philip sprinted out the door to have Miss Elsie call the ambulance. Mama started putting things in her purse. Mrs. Hernández continued monitoring Chich's temperature.

Soon Miss Elsie, Peewee, and the rest of the gang came over. Peewee ran into Mama's arms. Daddy appeared in the kitchen doorway, still in last night's shirt and trousers. "What's going on?" he said. "Why's everyone here?"

Mama walked into the kitchen, explaining Chich's condition to Daddy.

Chich patted my hand. "Regina, tell me a story. Stories have power."

"Which one?"

"The one about the beaver and the coyote."

"I don't know it that well." Water welled up in my eyes. "What if I tell it wrong?"

Chich smiled. "You won't."

I took a deep breath. My eyes darted around. Miss Elsie shooed the kids outside. Mama and Daddy now spoke quietly in a corner. Mrs. Hernández took Chich's temperature again.

I cleared my throat. "There once was a beaver that lived in a simple pond," I started. "Even though it was simple, Beaver thought his home was perfect . . ."

"Her temperature is rising . . . now one hundred and three degrees," Mrs. Hernández announced.

"One day," I went on, "Coyote came and

said, 'Beaver, I know of a better pond—'"

"Owww," moaned Chich, clutching her right side.

"Beaver, the pond that I speak of has water so clear you can see the bottom. There are many plants. More than you can possibly eat. I can take you to it if you want me to—"

"The girls won't be able to come to the hospital," Mama said to Miss Elsie.

"Beaver's wife told him, 'Do not go with Coyote. Our home is perfect for us.'"

"They can come over to my house," Miss Elsie replied. "The kids can play."

"But Beaver followed Coyote to see this more perfect place—"

Sirens blared down our street and stopped in front of our house. I continued, trying to talk faster. "Beaver followed Coyote past the mountains and valleys. Past the hills and rocks. So far did Beaver walk that he couldn't remember where his home was. At that moment, Coyote turned to eat Beaver. But Beaver dug a river up from the ground and swam quickly away—"

"Regina, you'll need to move, sweetheart," Mama urged.

I continued the story. "Beaver got away from Coyote—"

Two men dressed in white jackets had entered and headed toward Chich and me on the couch.

"He didn't know where he was. Beaver searched everywhere for his simple pond—"

"Hi there. Mind if I check your grand-mother?" asked one man, trying to place himself between me and Chich.

"I need to finish this story," I said, holding on to Chich's hand. She nodded for me to continue. "And to this day, beavers move from pond to pond, trying to find that perfect home Beaver left behind."

"Thank you," Chich said.

"Okay, Regina, you finished it. Let this man take care of Chich," Daddy said as he gently moved me away.

Mrs. Hernández explained what she'd observed to the second man. He nodded. "You a doctor?"

"Yes."

The first man took Chich's temperature again and held her wrist. Then he touched her stomach. She cried out.

"You're hurting her!" I said.

Daddy held me back. "She's in good hands, Regina."

"Don't hurt her!" I yelled.

The two men lifted Chich onto a gurney, and we all followed as they carried her to the ambulance outside. Most of our block on 58th Place watched the men in white jackets place her inside. Mrs. Hernández gave Mama a hug and gathered Philip and Anthony to walk home. Miss Elsie held Addie's and Peewee's hands as they stood on the lawn. Peewee whimpered.

"It's going to be all right," Miss Elsie said to Peewee.

I glanced at Keith from the porch, my cheeks damp, my breath heavy.

"My mama said you're coming to our house," Keith said as he jumped up next to me.

I just nodded and wiped my eyes to see Daddy

help Mama into the car. The ambulance drove off with its siren blaring. Daddy followed.

Keith shuffled his feet. Then he draped his arm around me. I tried to hold back more tears. "Come on, Regina. Let's go."

Later on, Miss Elsie got the call from Daddy at the hospital. Chich had died. Not from her appendix. The doctor told Daddy that the surgery had gone well.

But right after that, her heart gave out.

No one at the hospital knew about Chich's little white pills that she took for it.

And I couldn't help wondering if Daddy cutting my hair had taken Chich away from us.

26

UMPQUA ALWAYS

When Daddy and Mama got back from the hospital, our friends in the neighborhood gathered at our house. Miss Elsie comforted Mama. Then she hugged me and Peewee tight, cried with us, and told us how Chich went to heaven.

Keith didn't know what to say. He stood in silence, rocking slowly back and forth on his heels. Addie went over to hug Peewee, wailing with her.

Mr. Hernández and Mr. Bates stood by the television, talking in lowered voices with Daddy. Neighbors started bringing us food. Mrs.

Hernández brought over ropa vieja. Even Mrs. Gartner, who pretty much kept to herself, came over with streuselkuchen. Everyone seemed to feel as awful as we did.

Not quite two days later, I heard a loud sound rattling outside. I ran to the window and saw Cousin Harlin's pickup truck in front of our house.

Clad in a plaid shirt, faded blue jeans, and logging boots, he jumped out quick to help Aunt Rosie get out of the cab. They gathered food out of the pickup bed and headed for the front porch. I ran out to help.

"From your family," Cousin Harlin said to Daddy, handing over the bags as they came up the front porch. "Figured you needed some real food."

Daddy took the rest of the bags and handed one to Peewee as we went back in. The three of us set them on the kitchen table and peeked inside. Jars of huckleberry jam sat among the dried salmon and deer meat. Cousin Harlin hugged Daddy for a long time. Mama hugged Aunt

Rosie. Then Peewee and I got hugs from both of them.

Aunt Rosie didn't waste any time. "You need to bury her in Grand Ronde," she said directly to Daddy.

"We can't afford the expense of having her sent up there," he said matter-of-factly. "She has to be buried here."

"Then her spirit will wander."

Cousin Harlin cut in. "I could just wrap her up and throw her in the back of the pickup. No one would have to know," he offered. "Seriously, cuz, we can take her home."

Daddy had a slight smirk. Cousin Harlin always knew how to lighten up a hard situation.

"You need to bury her in Grand Ronde," Aunt Rosie said again. "Her spirit will wander if you don't."

Daddy had already gone to St. John's Catholic Church, where we'd attended Christmas Mass, to arrange Chich's funeral Mass. I had heard him talking to Mama about figuring out a burial site in Inglewood.

"The funeral Mass has already been arranged for tomorrow," Daddy said. "And it costs too much money to take her home."

Aunt Rosie studied Daddy. "I don't know what has come over you. But we're your family. We're here to help. Once you're from Grand Ronde, you're always from there. No matter where you live, how far away you go. Now, we'll have the funeral Mass tomorrow, but then she needs to go home. Our cemetery is still ours. That's where she belongs."

Daddy didn't respond, but I could see him mulling it over.

A knock at the door interrupted the discussion. Mrs. Hernández was back to take us girls over to St. John's to pray for Chich.

When we got up to the altar, I pushed a penny into the box next to the row of candles, picked up a stick, and lit a tiny candle. Peewee and I stood nearby as Mrs. Hernández knelt and said her prayer in Spanish.

After we got back, Keith stood outside our

house. "So are you going back home? My mom said you are."

I just stared at him, not sure what Miss Elsie and Mama had talked about while we were at church. "I am home," I said. "Chich is gone. Even if we get to take her home, how could I ever stay there by myself?"

As soon as I said it, I knew it was true. 58th Place had to be home—at least for now.

I no longer dreamed of Spirit Mountain every day or playing with my cousins in Yamhill Field. No sense in dreaming of something that couldn't come true. Now there was no one to continue teaching me how to be Umpqua.

I felt numb. And incredibly lost.

That feeling continued through the funeral Mass the next day and back at our house where everyone gathered to eat. Mama and Aunt Rosie cooked some of the food. We served venison stew, Portuguese bread with blackberry jam, and sausage. Miss Elsie brought over a baked ham and sweet potatoes. Mrs. Hernández brought arroz con pollo. And Peking's Restaurant delivered a lot of food too.

The adults sat in the house, talking and eating. Us kids ended up taking our plates and sitting outside on the front porch. But I couldn't eat anything.

By the time the sky grew dark, everyone headed home. We were all exhausted. I brushed my short hair and crawled into bed with Peewee. Aunt Rosie slept in Chich's bed.

Sometime in the middle of the night, the front door lock jiggled. I lifted my head to listen. After a few minutes, the door opened. Footsteps staggered through the living room into the kitchen. Deep mumbling echoed. Something crashed in the kitchen. Some cursing.

Then the back door slammed.

Curious, I slid off my bed. I crept through the dark living room and into the kitchen. Quietly flipping the overturned chair upright, I scooted it over to the window. I knelt on the seat and pulled away the window curtain to peer outside.

The full moon shone down. Scattered toys

and the garden hose sparkled under its light. The walnut tree glowed. Daddy, with his arms at his sides and head down, stood in the middle of the lawn. He was saying something.

Is he praying? I strained to listen.

A song traveled from the backyard. A familiar song.

"Aaaahhh . . . aiye . . . oooh . . ." Daddy sang and moved to the beat of the song. He stepped twice on each foot. His arms extended out. He twirled. He danced like they did back home. The old way.

"You should be in bed."

I whirled around. Cousin Harlin stood behind me, the scent of beer faint on his funeral suit. I hadn't heard him come inside.

I went back to watching Daddy from the kitchen window. "I didn't know Daddy knew the honor song," I said.

"'Course he knows the honor song," Cousin Harlin said as he peered out over my head. "He's Indian, after all. And we'll always be Indian, no matter how hard some of us try not to be."

"I want to stay Indian," I said.

"You will."

"But I don't have the rez to go back to. I don't have Chich. I don't have my tribal number."

"So?"

"So those things make you Indian."

"Regina, you were born Indian. Our family is Umpqua. Nothing changes that. Not the government. Not these city people. Not even that ole waitress who wouldn't serve you." Daddy must have told him about that.

I glanced back at the backyard. Daddy was still singing and dancing.

"Think I'll join him," Cousin Harlin said, hanging his black jacket over one of the chairs and walking to the back door. "By the way, we're all taking your chich home tomorrow. And . . . your ma is going to have a baby."

Then he opened the door, winked at me, and left.

Wait . . . we're really going to take Chich home?

And Mama's going to have a baby?

I wondered if Chich had known.

I stared out the window. Cousin Harlin and Daddy moved to the beat of their song, wailing in unison. Hopefully we could still have the traditional giveaway and all the singing for Chich like we did for Chup.

And Chich was right. We came from survivors. Our ancestors survived being forced to leave our homelands and march to Grand Ronde in the winter. Her mother overcame the loneliness and abuse in boarding school to return home and grow her own family. We had left Grand Ronde with five family members. In the end, we'd still be five.

I stared out the window again. Daddy was Indian. He wasn't hiding his heritage. He wasn't pretending to be something else. He knew Chich needed to go home and decided to make it happen.

And I knew when we returned, Daddy would drive to work wearing his black pants and tie, believing he would be accepted someday.

But tonight . . .

I thought about all I had been through. What

had Chich said once? All that you experienced, whether won or lost, was yours.

I was Indian even without my braids. I was Indian even if I didn't own a headdress or a pony. I was Indian even if I was Indian no more.

Because I knew where I came from.

Because I knew my Umpqua ancestors.

And because I survived to tell their stories and mine.

Like this one.

DEFINITIONS

Note: It is well known that "Indians" is not the correct term for Native Nations indigenous to the Western Hemisphere. Yet since Columbus, the misnomer has persisted over centuries. This historical novel takes place in the 1950s when "Indian" was the prevailing English word to describe tribes and their citizens, languages, and cultures. That is why the word is used by both the Umpqua characters in the book as well as those who are not.

The label is also reflected in the federal laws and policies of the era, i.e., the Indian Relocation Act, etc. The inaccurate term persists even today because of that historic use and the continuing presence of the federal Bureau of Indian Affairs and Indian Health Service in the lives of Native Nations and their citizens. Even in more recent times, some Native people, especially elders, use the word *Indian* to refer to themselves.

arroz con pollo: a simple dish originating in Spain featuring cooked chicken, tomatoes, herbs, and rice

Azores: a group of nine islands in the Atlantic Ocean west of Portugal that govern their own affairs separate from that country

BIA: an acronym for the Bureau of Indian Affairs within the United States Department of the Interior

catsup: a condiment made mostly from tomatoes and vinegar, now generally referred to as ketchup

Chinook (chah-nook) winds: strong, warm winter winds that blow inland off the Pacific Ocean

confirmation: a sacrament within the Catholic Church for older children or teens who were baptized as an infant or young child in the Church. It is a coming-of-age ceremony during which the child or teen makes a commitment to live out their faith.

Cowboys and Indians: a very common game for children in the 1950s to play, given the popularity of Westerns on television and in film. These media portrayed white cowboys fighting against and defeating Indians every time with rare exception. Given the problematic history of Indian-white relations that generations of children since then have learned about, the game is no longer played regularly.

elder: a term of respect used to refer to those of the older generations

giveaway: a large gathering typically of family, friends, and other community members that celebrates or commemorates someone's life or an important event. There is always a meal where everyone is fed. Gifts are also distributed to at least some of those attending to help them remember the person or occasion.

Hollywood Indians: stereotyped Native American characters created by the Hollywood movie and television industry. Usually played by white or other non-Native actors, speaking limited English as well as wearing wigs, makeup, and clothes that do not resemble any real Native people.

Indian agent: an assigned federal government worker who managed services provided by the federal government on the tribal reservations like Grand Ronde

Indian Relocation Act of 1956: a federal law aimed at relocating Native families from their reservation homes to cities such as Chicago, Denver, and Los Angeles, where they would receive job training and be assimilated into the general population. Many families and individuals from the Grand Ronde community participating in the program went to Seattle, Portland, San Francisco, and Los Angeles.

Injun (engine): a slang term for "Indian" used during the time period of this story, but which has not been acceptable for decades

lean-to: a simple structure supported on one side by trees to provide shelter from wind and rain

Long Bell Lumber Company: a white-owned logging company that once operated in Grand Ronde with additional mills elsewhere in the Pacific Northwest. It harvested mostly Douglas fir trees.

Lone Ranger: a fictional masked former lawman who tracked down outlaws in the western US with Tonto, his Indian sidekick. The show began on the radio in the 1930s, then launched novels, comic books, and finally a TV series from 1949–1957.

matador: a bullfighter

plankhouse: a wooden house, usually made of cedar, where traditionally many families lived under one roof. Today, community gatherings occur there. Also called a big house or a longhouse.

rez: a slang term for reservation

ropa vieja: a slow-cooked beef-and-vegetable stew served with rice, and one of the national dishes of Cuba

Spirit Mountain: the ancestral mountain range on the Grand Ronde reservation

stick game: a Native American guessing game played with two teams and multiple patterned sticks. The "hiding" team tries to distract the "guessing" team from naming the correct pattern on a stick held by a member of the hiding team, thereby keeping the sticks from being taken by the guessing team.

streuselkuchen: a German-style crumb cake

talk story: to tell a story verbally

termination: a federal policy that occurred from the 1940s through the 1960s. The US Congress passed a series of laws during this time that terminated—or ended—the government-to-government relationship between the United States and those Native Nations listed in the law.

This meant the end of the federal government providing services like health care, education, and other support as promised in the treaties signed by the US and the tribal leaders. In 1954, Congress voted for Public Law 588, which specifically terminated all of the tribes within The Confederated Tribes of Grand Ronde Community and other tribes in Oregon. President Eisenhower signed it into law. The Bureau of Indian Affairs fully implemented the law in Oregon two years after its enactment.

Three Stooges: a slapstick comedy team that formed in the vaudeville era of the 1920s and made black-and-white short films of their physical antics and jokes, which were later shown on television for decades

tipi: a cone-shaped portable living space made from animal skins tied over long poles. Tipis are the traditional homes of some Native Nations who traveled across the plains of North America.

Tonto: the fictional Apache sidekick who saved the Lone Ranger's life after a shootout with outlaws who killed the lawman's fellow Texas Rangers. Tonto assisted the Lone Ranger in catching the bad guys across the West. White actors voiced Tonto in the radio series, but

Jay Silverheels, a Mohawk actor from Canada, played the role in the popular TV series. At a time when many non-Natives played the part of Indians on TV, some Native American viewers were happy to see a Mohawk actor in the role, but his stoic demeanor and broken English also perpetuated old stereotypes about Native peoples.

tribal rolls: originally created by the US government to document Indians on reservations. Native Americans were assigned numbers based on blood count and tribal affiliation.

Umpqua (uhmp-kwah): Several different tribes from the southern portion of the Pacific Northwest who were forcibly removed to the Grand Ronde area of what is now known as the Willamette Valley. The federal government created the Grand Ronde Confederacy, grouping nearly thirty different Native Nations into one large governing body all living together on the Grand Ronde Indian Reservation.

AUTHOR'S NOTE

Dear Reader,

Although Regina is a fictional character in a historical novel, federal termination laws were real. They had a detrimental impact on many Native American children and families in Native Nations from coast to coast from the 1940s through the 1960s. These tribes found their government-to-government relationship with the United States severed when Congress passed those laws.

Like Regina, I lived for a while on The Confederated Tribes of the Grand Ronde reservation. However, I was one year old when my Umpqua tribe was terminated. I don't remember much about that time, only what family and tribal members passed down to me.

One tribal member said it best: "There was no Chinuk Wawa word for *termination* except for mimǝlust·ˣ." That means "to die" in my Native

House on 58th Place, Los Angeles, California

Charlene (second from left) and her sister (far right) with friends, Los Angeles, California

language. For many, this loss of identity was exactly how they felt. They had become the walking dead.

Along with termination, Congress passed the Indian Relocation Act in 1956. This removed many more Native people from their reservation homelands and relocated them to big cities like Chicago, Minneapolis, Denver, San Francisco, and Los Angeles. The government promised moving costs, jobs, higher education, and housing. Tens of thousands of Native people entered urban cities across the US.

My family opted for Los Angeles. Below is a photo of my sister and me in our new home on

58th Place, when we were younger than Regina and Peewee.

Charlene (left) and her younger sister, Los Angeles, California

Charlene standing next to the family car with her mother and sister,
Los Angeles, California

Charlene's father
serving in the navy in
World War II

Dugout Canoe Project at The Confederated Tribes of the Grand Ronde Community

Base of Spirit Mountain, The Confederated Tribes of the Grand Ronde Community

While living in Los Angeles, my sister and I did have friends upon whom I based the characters of Keith and Addie in the book. I have many photos of us posing for the camera, whether we were in our Halloween costumes or just playing around. Philip and Anthony are based on real brothers from Cuba who entertained the neighborhood kids with their circuses, magic shows, and marionette theater.

The memories of my time on 58th Place are mostly pleasant.

Charlene as a teen

Later, in 1968, President Lyndon B. Johnson addressed Congress with his "Forgotten Americans" speech, requested their help in funding education, employment, and health care programs, and instructed federal agencies to build better relationships with Indian tribes. Terminated tribes began meeting with Congressional members about restoring their trust

Traci Sorell

Community plankhouse at The Confederated Tribes of the Grand Ronde Community

Traci Sorell

▲ UMPQUA
▲ ROGUE RIVER
▲ CHASTA
▲ MOLALLA
▲ KALAPUYA

Veterans Memorial statue at The Confederated Tribes of the Grand
Ronde Community

Top of Spirit Mountain at The Confederated Tribes of the Grand Ronde Community

Charlene at The Confederated Tribes of the Grand Ronde Community

relationship. The Menominee Tribe in Wisconsin was the first tribe to have its status restored when, in 1973, Congress passed a bill which then-President Richard Nixon signed into law. This led to more tribes meeting with and testifying before Congress about how the termination law had devastated their governments, economies, and the lives of their citizens.

On November 22, 1983, after nearly thirty years of termination, President Reagan signed House Resolution 3885, also known as Public Law 98-365. That law restored The Confederated Tribes of the Grand Ronde Community as a federally recognized Tribe.

After that, Regina Petit and I became Indian once more.

—Charlene Willing McManis (1953–2018)

CO-AUTHOR'S NOTE

I first met Charlene Willing McManis in New York City at *Kweli Journal*'s The Color of Children's Literature Conference in 2016, where writers and illustrators of color and from Native Nations gather with literary agents and publishing professionals to learn, discuss craft, and network. Charlene and I visited about our work and backgrounds over lunch, so I came to know about this book she was writing. We stayed in contact after the conference. I interviewed her for Cynthia Leitich Smith's children's and young adult lit industry blog, *Cynsations*, when the formal announcement came out that Tu Books, an imprint of Lee & Low Books, had acquired her manuscript. We looked forward to seeing each other again at the 2018 Kweli Conference.

But that reunion never took place. Charlene had had cancer previously, and though she had successfully completed her treatments, the cancer returned. When she reached out to me to ask if I would consider revising and polishing her novel for publication, I felt honored and also ill-equipped. Who was I to do this work? I'm a citizen of the Cherokee Nation and not from The Confederated Tribes of Grand Ronde Community (CTGRC). I'd written picture books and poems, not middle-grade prose. So I took some time to pray, consider, and consult others. My literary agent, Emily Mitchell, read the manuscript and told me unequivocally that she believed I could do this. Charlene certainly believed I could, as did Stacy Whitman, publisher of Tu Books.

I accepted Charlene's request and still feel humbled to have done so. This book is the result of many years of hard work on her part to develop her craft in fiction writing, document-ing her Umpqua family's stories, interviewing fellow Grand Ronde tribal members about their experiences, and slogging through the many drafts to hone a story into the finished product you just read. It deserves to be in the world, shining a light on a very difficult period for many Native Nations and their citizens within the United States. While in the book Regina's father desired to leave Grand Ronde for what he believed were better opportunities off the reservation, that idea was not widely held by those who relocated through the federal program. Most left their tribal homelands with a heavy heart, although driven by the same desire her father has in the book to provide for their families and themselves.

To that end, I have worked not just to refine and polish Charlene's story for publication, but to help with its historical accuracy. No work can ever be perfect. But a historical novel highlighting real federal policies of removal, termination, and relocation as they impact an actual Native nation needs to be as correct as possible. There is also information about language and culture shared in this book that had to be vetted.

I'm grateful to Lee & Low for its invaluable support in sending me to visit the CTGRC Cultural Resources Department. The staff generously gave of their time, expertise, and resources. They provided me with a Chinuk Wawa dictionary, other books to take with me for reference, and admission to their research holdings to view photos, maps, and other printed materials I would never have had easy access to otherwise. I want to thank the department manager David Harrelson and his staff, especially Bobby Mercier, Jordan Mercier, Sibyl Edwards, Julie Brown, Briece Edwards, and Cheryl Pouley, for the time they spent answering my questions and pointing me to other source materials I needed. Those first five individuals listed also read the novel and provided feedback, which helped my revision process immensely. To all of you, masi, as they say in Chinuk Wawa.

That said, any errors or misrepresentations of the CTGRC, its physical location, history, culture, or language are solely attributable to Charlene and me as the coauthors of this fictional work. For ease of use, all of Chich's words are presented in Chinuk Wawa, not Umpqua. Since Chinuk Wawa is the language taught and used by CTGRC members in their schools, communities, and ceremonies, the book reflects this contemporary usage.

Despite all the Grand Ronde people have been through, they have survived and continue to thrive. Their cemetery, as mentioned in the story, never left the tribe's control even after termination. It was key in their restoration, providing a lasting connection to their land as people continued to be brought home and buried there after 1954.

Today, after restoration of their tribal status, the CTGRC have developed a variety of successful business ventures that help support their educational, cultural, and infrastructure priorities for their citizens. I had the honor of visiting their Chachalu Museum and seeing items they had recently received on loan from the British Museum in London. It's no small feat to have the necessary facility, resources, staff, and vision to pull off such a complicated logistical and diplomatic exchange of important cultural materials across continents. I am in awe of the work the Tribe is doing to keep its citizens connected to their culture and language, both within the community as well as online.

I also extend my appreciation to Christopher Hill, Facilities Services Division, Los Angeles Unified School District, for providing photographs of the historic Budlong Avenue Elementary School building featured in this story.

I have my own community to thank as well. There are no words to express the depth of my gratitude for Charlene's family, especially her husband Roger, for clarifications, photos, and support throughout this entire process while dealing with their difficult loss. Because of this book, we will be connected forever as part of her legacy. I appreciate the assistance provided by Charlene's cousin, Leroy Good, and his wife, Mary Ellen, directing me toward additional sources for the book. Wado to Elise McMullen-Ciotti, my editor and fellow Cherokee Nation citizen, whose support and feedback made this book stronger.

While Spanish is my second language, I wanted to make sure what dialogue I attributed to Mrs. Hernández would be realistic for a

Cuban woman to say. Gracias a Margarita Engle, award-winning Cuban poet and Charlene's mentor through We Need Diverse Books, who reviewed those passages for me and guided Charlene in strengthening her story for submission.

I would not be an author at all without the love and flexibility of my entire family. My husband Mark and my mother Carolyn fact-checked many items for me, read the manuscript aloud, and helped proofread it. They, along with my son, endure my long hours crafting stories and poems. I love and cherish them immensely.

—Traci Sorell

EDITOR'S NOTE

How I came to have Charlene's manuscript in my hands seems like a miracle.

At the time, I was transitioning from many years working in marketing at a large publishing house into freelance editorial work. I wasn't sure where I would land or if I still wanted to work in publishing. I had struggled as a Cherokee within the publishing industry. Why couldn't we move beyond marketing Native American books only in November and around the Thanksgiving holiday? Why were the only Native stories ever given voice frozen within the mid-nineteenth century? The answer I usually received when asking these questions was that there was no market for Native stories. Since we represented such a small amount of the population, and since most publishing houses believed only Native Americans would read them, there wasn't really a demand for our stories. They were just not worth the investment.

Yet the winds changed. Through a contact at the Society of Children's Book Writers and Illustrators (SCBWI), Adria Quinones, I learned that Stacy Whitman at Tu Books was looking for a Native American editor. She needed someone to do an expert read on a Native middle-grade novel. We connected by email, and she sent me *Indian No More*. The writer had submitted the novel to the New Visions Award contest. It was not developed or structured enough to win the award, but the committee saw that it had something special.

I was glad to hear that it was written by a Native writer, Charlene Willing McManis. I'd been asked to do sensitivity reading before, and more times than not, the stories were not written by Native writers, and I'd have to inform the editors that these were not honest or accurate books. So I was excited to dig in to a hopefully authentic piece. I printed it out, stapled it together, and began reading. I didn't stop until I was done . . . except to take a few minutes here and there to cry.

Up to that point in my publishing career, no one had ever talked about the Indian termination policies or the additional and continual migrations of Native people throughout the country for survival. *Indian No More* reminded me of the late Cherokee Nation Chief Wilma Mankiller and her family's relocation to San Francisco in 1956—and her return to Oklahoma in 1977. It also reminded me of when my grandmother returned to Oklahoma after living in Dallas for so long. I was happy for her but sad when she left us behind in Texas. These stories of forced movement and survival and reclamation are rare out in the world. I felt seen.

Holding Charlene's manuscript in my hands seemed sacred. I proceeded to call my mother, my grandmother, and my Native friends, telling them about the story I had just read and reading them certain excerpts. I wrote my report. It was insistent. It stated that this was a story that had to be published. It needed work, but it also needed to be out in the world.

After sending in my report, I continued to

check in about the novel. Was Tu Books going to publish it? About six months later, it was decided: *Indian No More* would see the light of day. I was ecstatic.

Soon after, I was invited to be a part of the 2018 New Visions Award Writing contest. The day we voted on the winner, I was pulled aside and told that Charlene was ill and in hospice. I was greatly saddened by the news. Stacy reassured me that Tu was still going to publish the book and that Charlene had asked her friend and fellow writer Traci Sorell to pick up the edits where she left off, to bring it fully into the world. Traci is a fellow citizen of the Cherokee Nation. We began a dialogue shortly after Charlene's passing and funeral.

A month or so later, Stacy asked if I would be the co-editor of the book. I went home and sat with that invitation. On the one hand, it would be a giant honor. On the other hand, I knew that this work would hold a great deal of responsibility.

What many non-Natives do not realize is that it is very rare for us to "get the microphone" within society. And when we do, we are very, very aware of all the Native Americans standing with us. We speak for ourselves as individuals—we all have a voice—but we are never speaking only for ourselves. We are speaking for a much larger group on some level: our family, our community, our tribal nation, and the greater nations at large. We feel the responsibility to get it right the first time, because we might not get that microphone again for a long time . . . if ever.

So with great honor, I said yes.

Books are published all the time. There are giant machines that have been in place for centuries to put stories out on shelves or in magazines and newspapers. Yet Native people do things differently. We value relationships above financial outcomes. We take time in making our decisions. We are always seeking the best for the group and not just the individual. I had in my hands a number of people to make sure to honor: There was Charlene, her husband Roger, and her family; Charlene's Native friends and community in Vermont; the people of Grand Ronde; our new writer, Traci Sorell; her family, my family, our Cherokee Nation, the larger Native American population, and all of our collective ancestors. There was also the African American community, since our story takes place during the Civil Rights era, and our protagonist's closest friends are Black Americans. Oh, yes . . . and the people of Tu Books and Lee & Low.

Traci and I set about the work. Our first editorial meeting was held on October 14, 2018 in New York City, on what was formerly Columbus Day. She then headed back to Oklahoma to get to work. With my first editorial notes, a box of Charlene's research and notes, and Charlene's original manuscript, Traci began developing and writing the next draft. We went back and forth with it, preparing it—not for Tu Books, but for Traci's trip to The Confederated Tribes of the Grand Ronde Community (CTGRC) in Oregon. Traci and I are Cherokee. We were (and are still) no authority on Grand Ronde or Umpqua history. Charlene too had planned to seek out elders and culture keepers at the reservation to go over her manuscript. Unfortunately, Charlene didn't have the chance for that final trip to Grand Ronde. Now Traci was going in Charlene's stead, retracing her footsteps and filling in the blanks. David Harrelson, the department manager, and his team spent several days generously giving of their time working with her.

While Traci was there, Stacy and I met to discuss the cover. Traci had shared with us a list of Native American illustrators and artists to consider. In the end, we felt that the work of Marlena Myles (Spirit Lake Dakota, Mohegan, Muscogee Creek) would be perfect for *Indian No More*. Stacy reached out to see if she would do it. We received a yes.

A few weeks later, I traveled to Vermont to meet with Charlene's family and friends. I had never had the opportunity to meet Charlene in person, and if I was going to honor her, her family, and her adopted Native community there, I needed to hear some stories—to get to know Charlene in any way I could. We met on a snowy day in Montpelier. Sarah Rosenthal, a friend of

Charlene's, had offered her office, a large con-
verted Victorian home, for our meeting. I
knew we would have elders coming, so we
set up the room with chairs in a circle. We
would do this the Native way. For four hours,
we went around the circle, sharing all we
wanted to share about Charlene and the story
she had written. I received permission to take
notes and asked questions from time to time.
Abenaki, Shoshone, Cherokee, and non-Native
allies lifted Charlene, an Umpqua, up in story
that day.

Coincidentally (or maybe more serendipi-
tously), Traci was also in Vermont that weekend. She arranged for us to have dinner with
Charlene's husband Roger McManis, Charlene's daughter Sarah, and her granddaughter.
Again we lifted up Charlene in story. Roger
played us a voice mail message of Charlene
being excited at a writing event because her
story had received some attention. Her voice
was light and happy, vivacious and fun. We
shared with Roger and Sarah where we were

with the book. We also asked questions. Charlene had based much of *Indian No More* on her
own childhood, and we wanted to make sure
we were writing and editing authentically.
They shared with us more photos, more stories, and we left content yet melancholy, feeling the loss of Charlene.

Meanwhile, Marlena had been working on
the cover art. We had sent her images Traci
had taken while in CTGRC so that she could
incorporate the proper cultural elements onto
the cover. Marlena had also been very clear
about what she thought of the story and what
she thought it needed for the greater Native
community. Her voice was welcome.

Soon Traci, Stacy, and I were in final edits
of the manuscript. We debated some on what
was needed to flesh out the last details, taking
the time to do so, not only because that's what
birthing a novel is like, but because we had an
additional challenge. We couldn't just call Charlene up and ask, "What did you mean by this?"
or "What would you like to do?" So what was

 203

right? Was it just anyone's guess? In the end, we came to some wonderful, simple solutions.

Again, this draft of the manuscript would not be the last. It would need to go back to CTGRC. There was no way we would move forward without their cultural advisors' check on what was written. It had to be absolutely culturally correct. It would also go to an African American reader to check our African American characters' truths and authenticity.

Meanwhile, Stacy, Marlena, and I were going through several renditions of the cover. How would we create something completely Native, honor everyone involved, and still fit today's predominantly white cultural idea of "what sells" as far as book covers go? We needed to honor the artist, CTGRC, Umpqua culture, *and* the story—plus market it in a way that made non-Native and Native readers alike want to buy it. Not easy. And it wasn't. But in the end, we succeeded. Marlena created beautiful, authentic art for the cover. If you look at the trees and mountains, you will see Native symbols from CTGRC. The trees have symbols meaning "fingers and hands," and the mountains have symbols meaning "fishing spears." We sent the art to CTGRC. All was good.

Now we had everything, and our amazing book designer began assembling our work. We still had to go through the process of copyediting, of interior page design, of marketing, of advanced reading copies, of getting this book into readers' hands. But we could breathe now. We had done it the Native way. We had done our absolute best to honor that big paragraph of people I wrote about earlier in this note.

We were given a microphone. I hope we used it well.

Working as an editor for *Indian No More* has been a sacred journey. I am truly grateful for every single person who stood with me and walked with me through this process. I am grateful to Stacy Whitman, publisher of Tu Books, who entrusted me with this beautiful project. I am grateful to Jason Low, Cheryl Klein, and Hannah Ehrlich at Lee & Low Books, who generously gave of their time and expertise. Lee & Low and Tu Books continue to make it part of their mission to find and publish Native American stories— and kidlit is better for it.

I am grateful to Charlene's friends who shared their time with me: Sarah Rosenthal, Kathy Quimby Johnson, Sean Anderson, Kate Ross, and elders Patty Manning (Abenaki), Jeanne A. Brink and her husband (Abenaki), and Laura Callahan (Shoshone). I am grateful to The Confederated Tribes of the Grand Ronde Community, and especially David Harrelson and his team.

I am grateful to Roger McManis, Charlene's husband, and their daughter Sarah for being our touchstone to Charlene whenever we needed it. I am also grateful to Traci, my fellow Cherokee, and an amazing force of a writer, who held steadfast in authenticity with every beautiful word.

I am grateful to my own family and friends who read drafts and gave notes, especially my Cherokee mother and grandmother, Liz Mullen and Sarah Burchardt, my sister Margaret

Wood, and Jenna Boatman, who all have been cheering this project on as we walked the journey. I am grateful for my husband, Lenny Ciotti, who always whispered in my ear, "You can do this."

And finally, I am grateful for Charlene. Thank you, Charlene, for this story and for your Umpqua heart. Wado.

—Elise McMullen-Ciotti

THE BEAVER AND THE COYOTE

There once was a beaver that lived in a simple pond. Even though it was simple, Beaver thought his home was perfect.

One day, Coyote came and said, "Beaver, I know of a better pond where the water is so clear, you can see the bottom. There are many plants. More than you can possibly eat. I can take you to it if you want me to."

Beaver's wife told him, "Do not go with Coyote. Our home is perfect for us." But Beaver followed Coyote to see this more perfect place, past the mountains and valleys. Past the hills and rocks. So far did Beaver walk that he couldn't remember where his home was. At that moment, Coyote turned to eat Beaver. But Beaver dug a river up from the ground and swam quickly away.

Beaver got away from Coyote, but now he didn't know where he was. He searched everywhere for his simple pond. And to this day, beavers move from pond to pond, trying to find that perfect home that was left behind.

OUR AUTHORS

The late **CHARLENE WILLING MCMANIS** (1953-2018) was born in Portland, Oregon and grew up in

Los Angeles. She was of Umpqua tribal heritage and enrolled in The Confederated Tribes of Grand Ronde. Charlene served in the US Navy and later received her Bachelor's degree in Native American Education. She lived with her family in Vermont and served on that state's Commission on Native American Affairs. In 2016, Charlene received a mentorship with award-winning poet and author Margarita Engle through We Need Diverse Books. That manuscript became this novel, which is based on her family's experiences after their tribe was terminated in 1954. She passed away in 2018, knowing that her friend Traci Sorell would complete the revisions Charlene was unable to finish.

TRACI SORELL writes fiction and nonfiction books as well as poems for children. *We Are Grateful:*

Otsaliheliga ᎠᎬᏓᎵᎮᎵᎦ, her Sibert Honor–, Boston Globe/Horn Book Honor–, and Orbis Pictus Honor–award-winning nonfiction picture book, received starred reviews from *Kirkus Reviews*, *School Library Journal*, *The Horn*

Book and *Shelf Awareness*. A former federal Indian law attorney and policy advocate, she is an enrolled citizen of the Cherokee Nation and lives in northeastern Oklahoma, where her tribe is located. For more about Traci and her other works, visit tracisorell.com.